Praise for TONY DUNB
the Tubby Dubonnet series:

"The literary equivalent of a *film noir* – fast, tough, tense, and darkly funny…so deeply satisfying in the settling of the story's several scores that a reader might well disturb the midnight silence with laughter."
—*Los Angeles Times Book Review*

"Hair-Raising… Dunbar revels in the raffish charm and humor of his famously rambunctious city."
—*The New York Times Book Review*

"From the Bywater … to Uptown, Tubby eats and drinks his way through interrogations and rendezvous, and it's all delicious. Packed with contemporary New Orleans culture and plenty of humor from the quirky characters."
—*New Orleans Advocate*

"Reminiscent of the best of Donald Westlake and Elmore Leonard."
—*Booklist*

"Solidly put together. Dunbar's understated, syncopated delivery makes you wonder if there are enough honest men in New Orleans for a rubber of bridge."
—*Kirkus Reviews*

"An enjoyable romp through a city that makes Los Angeles seem normal."
—*San Francisco Chronicle*

"Sharp and jolly ... There's a lot here to enjoy – especially some great moments in local cuisine and a wonderfully jaundiced insider's view of a reluctant lawyer in action."

—*Chicago Tribune*

"For all the eccentric characters and bizarre events that Dunbar stuffs into his colorful narrative, the story holds up in court."

—*New York Times Book Review*

FLAG BOY

A Tubby Dubonnet Mystery

BY

TONY DUNBAR

booksBnimble Publishing
New Orleans, La.

Flag Boy

Copyright © 2017 by Tony Dunbar

This book is available in both mobi and print formats.

eBook ISBN: 978-0-9973630-6-7
Print ISBN-13: 978-0-9973630-7-4

www.booksbnimble.com

First booksBnimble electronic publication: September, 2017

Print layout by eBooks By Barb for Booknook.biz

Table of Contents

Dedication 7

PREFACE 9
CHAPTER 1 13
CHAPTER 2 17
CHAPTER 3 23
CHAPTER 4 35
CHAPTER 5 39
CHAPTER 6 41
CHAPTER 7 45
CHAPTER 8 51
CHAPTER 9 59
CHAPTER 10 67
CHAPTER 11 71
CHAPTER 12 75
CHAPTER 13 81
CHAPTER 14 87
CHAPTER 15 93
CHAPTER 16 99
CHAPTER 17 107
CHAPTER 18 109
CHAPTER 19 121
CHAPTER 20 129
CHAPTER 21 135
CHAPTER 22 141
CHAPTER 23 147
CHAPTER 24 153
CHAPTER 25 157
CHAPTER 26 163
CHAPTER 27 167
CHAPTER 28 179
CHAPTER 29 187
CHAPTER 30 193

How About A Free Book? 195
Guarantee 196
A Respectful Request 196
Also by Tony Dunbar 198
About the Author 199

Dedication

To John Henry, Annalisa, and Sam, the next generation

PREFACE

A slim woman whose golden hair was tied back by rose-colored clips, and her partner, a taller, broader woman, got out of a beat-up Toyota on a quiet side street in Uptown New Orleans. They walked swiftly down the dark block, passing run-down office buildings, vacant lots, and worn-out shotgun houses, without conversing. The streetlights were buried in the hackberry trees that had gotten out of control along the curb, and there were no signs of life in the houses. It was two hours past midnight, and both women had, for the past couple of hours, been drinking wine. Approaching Napoleon Avenue, they stepped off the sidewalk to huddle beside a two-story medical building, close against the wall, as if they were sharing a smoke or a kiss.

Both women were in very good shape, which was why the larger one could make a cup with her hands, hoist her friend onto her shoulders, and steady her there by her ankles. And with a hissed command, she flung her somersaulting into the air to land miraculously on the narrow concrete ledge, no more than eight inches deep, below a double window on the second floor. This was quite a remarkable feat, had anyone been around to see it. The gymnast tossed down a soft nylon rope, and her big partner was up it as fast as a snake.

Perched on one foot the small acrobat dexterously pulled a plastic shim from a pack belted to her waist and slid it under the top window sash. She found the latch as if it were as familiar to her as the clasp of her own purse and had it open. Using a tiny razor to trace the window's outline, she cut through the bead of accumulated paint. Then she edged away so that her partner, with her superior strength, could force the window up. A sudden rush of air conditioning welcomed them into the doctor's office.

"Here's where they all sit and wait for him," the small woman whispered and let her pencil flashlight play over the chairs, the table full of Vogues, Southern Livings, and glossy New Orleans magazines – and over the tasteful, peaceful seascapes hanging on the walls. The paintings depicted domestic content and beautiful female sunbathers, mothers on vacation. Their children, playing in the sand, were happy and blond. "Here's where they wait for him to cut them up for dinner."

This woman did not always make perfect sense, but her partner was used to that. "A real son of a bitch," she agreed, under her breath.

Silently the blonde tested the door to the examination rooms and found it locked. Rather than fool with it, she slid herself through the portal behind which, in the daytime, a receptionist would sit to greet patients. She opened the door from the inside. There was the faint sound of reggae music coming from the wall speakers, a sound system that was never completely turned off. The passageway led to a large room blacked out completely from the world outside.

"Here's where he does it to you," she said. There were pastel pictures on the wall here also. And comfortable chairs and lamps to read by. And in the middle of the room was the long table, wrapped in expensive and soft white sheets and blankets, where the devil had operated on her.

"Nice set up," her friend whispered.

"Yeah," the fair-haired woman said. "Really nice. Let's find those pictures."

They found the filing cabinets, with wide drawers that glowed pink and lavender in the flashlights, in the next room. They were locked but yielded quickly to a tiny pick from the magic pouch. The small woman began rifling through them, looking for her name. Her friend also searched, more methodically.

There was a noise outside. It was the elevator coming to life. They heard it stop. The doors on their floor opened. "Shit," the intruders whispered in unison.

It was a night watchman making his rounds. The bigger of the pair instantly leapt to the ceiling, securing herself by a toe-hold on the top of the doorframe and two fingertips on an overhead light. This was pretty amazing, but she did it. The small one curled into a file drawer and closed herself in. Who would have thought a woman's body could do that?

They heard the front door of the office open and saw the lights in the other room switch on. They didn't breathe.

In a few moments, the lights went off and the entrance door slammed shut. One burglar popped off the ceiling and landed like a cat. The other unfurled from her cabinet. They went back to work – with more urgency this time – rifling through piles of documents and letting them spill onto the floor.

"They're not here," the small woman said finally. "The bastard keeps me somewhere else." She looked over the heap of paper they had created. "Let's get out of here," she said.

"Do we leave this mess?" her partner asked.

"Why not? It will give them something to worry about. They deserve it."

They left the way they had come, silently, and latched the window from the outside so that no one would ever figure this out. They dropped to the street, no louder than falling leaves, and floated away into the night.

CHAPTER 1

Prince Bazaar and his entourage arrived at Concourse A of Louis Armstrong International Airport on a direct flight from London. The group had been inspected carefully at each security checkpoint along the way and had attracted much attention on the plane, due largely to their exotic appearance.

The Prince himself wore a flowing robe and keffiyeh, which covered much of his forehead. It was held in place by a black rope circlet. A golden medallion in the center represented a coiled snake. Above his starched collar was a pointy beard and a thin black mustache, but his face, which was visible, was tanned, relaxed, and youthful. A woman followed closely behind him and intently fingered the back of his tunic, as if holding a tether. She was vividly covered in a long purple shawl with a fashionable blue hijab around her hair, all a little bit wrinkled from the long flight. She was quite fatigued, but she hid it well. Behind her came two other women so well-concealed by their billowing garments that their faces, figures, and ages were purely guesswork. Underneath their robes, which were a charming pale shade of green, both women were in their early twenties and quite beautiful. On their invisible heels was a pair of young men with bushy black hair and faces too young for razors wearing identical creamy white Italian suits. Their tapered, uncuffed pants ended ankle-high, revealing black shoes of Tuscan leather. Finally, two fair-skinned youths came pulling two roller-bags apiece. Cultivated muscles were well displayed through tight Armani T-shirts and skin-hugging jeans.

Once they passed beyond security and emerged into the lobby, the party was immediately greeted by a thin and dapper man with an effervescent smile. He rushed up to them overflowing with enthusiasm.

"Hello, your Highness!" the man proclaimed in a high voice, "and welcome to my city." E.J. Chaisson made a grand sweeping gesture with both hands, as if to show that all of New Orleans was his to lay before the feet of these esteemed newcomers. "I'm sure you must have luggage. Please, please, let me help you!"

Indeed they did have luggage at the baggage claim carousel, and it took two redcaps with large wheeled carts to transport it. During the time it took to get all of their suitcases and trunks assembled, E.J. called Uber, having quickly recognized that the mini-van he was driving couldn't handle the job of carrying this vast household to the city. The Prince thanked E.J. for meeting them, and the genetically effusive French Quarter landlord assured the new arrivals, repeatedly, that everything was well arranged for their comfort.

"We're ready to party, you might say," the Prince reported as they exited through the sliding glass doors into reassuringly familiar heat.

"Monsieur, it's in the bag," E.J. promised happily. His visitor smiled, though he wasn't familiar with that particular expression.

The local man took the lead of what had become a small caravan. He cruised down Interstate 10 with Prince Bazaar seated beside him and the woman in the purple shawl, whom he introduced as "my wife, my faithful wife," in the back. Following them very closely was a white stretch limo carrying the rest of the entourage and all of the luggage.

"I will have the house all ready for your inspection first thing in the morning," E.J. told the Prince as they went under the Causeway. "If everything is in order, and I'm sure it is, you can move over tomorrow."

"I know it will all be fine," the Prince said pleasantly, and certainly it should be. He had put down a huge deposit on a three-story historic house on a French Quarter corner, with wrap-around balconies surrounding both the second and third floors and wrought iron railings all about. Within was a ballroom, the master's living quarters, an enormous chef's kitchen, baths with extraordinarily expensive faucets, bidets, and appliances, and at least nine bedrooms. "Where are we going now?" his Highness inquired.

"Temporary quarters at a hotel, the Windsor Court. I was sure you would all like an afternoon to rest after your long journey."

"Does it have a sauna, a pool, a bar?"

"Of course it has a sauna and a very nice pool, and every place imaginable in New Orleans has a bar."

"That's good," the Prince nodded. "Let's, uh ... get it on," he added, trying out a new phrase.

"Right on." E.J. glowed. He had to stop himself from elbowing the Prince in the ribs.

After successfully depositing the crowd in the hotel lobby,

turning them over to the hovering concierge, and seeing that they had quite satisfactory rooms – an entire floor of them, in fact – E.J. collected his mini-van from the hotel valet. He gave the man a lovely tip.

After humming a little song to himself, *Happy Birthday to me*, he said out loud, "I've got to call Tubby right away and get him to write up a lease."

CHAPTER 2

Tubby Dubonnet, E.J.'s lawyer, didn't pick up when E.J. phoned. He wasn't even in the city.

Instead he was floating in the gently rippling solitude of Boley Creek, a sleepy river that ran through a sandy woodland in Mississippi. It was property he had bought back when he had a few bucks, as an investment, but mainly to chill out on occasion. At the moment he was lying comfortably on an inflated inner tube, held in place by some clothesline tied to a log, and he was staring at an uncomplicated sky. Sunlight sparkled through the tangle of overhanging limbs where dragonflies flitted about with tiny buzzes. He was thinking over the events he had experienced in the past few weeks. Events that, whichever direction he ran the tape, culminated in the unsolved murder by shotgun of a vicious retired cop named Kronke.

In Tubby's dream, he had pulled the trigger. There had been a great blast, a shattered windshield, and a bleeding headless man crumpled in the driver's seat.

To explain his departure from the city, the attorney had concocted a series of stories. He told his girlfriend Peggy that he had pressing legal business in Mississippi, which might take a week or two. She was understanding. He told his secretary

17

Cherrylynn that he had family matters to attend to in north Louisiana and might be gone for a month. She was thrilled at his industry. He let his daughters know that he needed a vacation and would check in on them just as soon as he could. They took little notice.

The truth was that he needed to leave town for pressing personal reasons – summed up as getting his mind right.

It was winter in the rest of the country, but it was one of the most beautiful times of the year near the Gulf of Mexico. Cool breezes, blue skies, not too many mosquitos, no rain – perfect for taking refuge, camping out in the woods of Pearl River County, Mississippi. He had just wanted himself for company. His provisions were bacon and coffee and eggs, a loaf of rye bread, an ice chest, and some beer. Not a menu for fun, but for soul searching.

He had driven his green 1967 Corvette Roadster, with the fake black leather interior, north on I-59, a cup of CC's coffee gripped in one hand. A lunatic car dealer named Lucky Lafrene had convinced him to trade in his Camaro and invest his life savings in this 300 HP V-8 collector's item. Its convertible top only leaked when it rained and the plastic rear window was only slightly smoky. The troubled lawyer piloted his green machine through long stretches of pine forest where eagles soared overhead and 18-wheelers whizzed by, and then off the main highway and into the brooding countryside.

Tubby had often been in proximity to crimes of violence, but the recent slaying of the sadistic and menacing retired lawman, Paul Kronke, had seriously unnerved him. And it was all because of those damn Cubans.

There was, he had learned to his dismay and imperilment, a

crazy band of old freedom fighters and their grandkids who were under the misguided impression that Tubby cared a whoop about their underground mission, their huge cache of arms, their dwindling but still substantial stash of money, and their possible link to the assassination of John F. Kennedy. Their secret mission had begun as the overthrow of Castro, but it had morphed into resisting worldwide socialism, and morphed again into aspiring to be the vanguard of the armed alt-right. The now-deceased cop was supposedly the band's enforcer.

Tubby had not a single mite of interest in any of the foregoing, but nonetheless the frightening goons had terrorized him, his family, and his girlfriend – even trying to kill them. That's just how crazy the world could be.

Over time, the threats became way too real. Tubby Dubonnet was a lawyer, a respected professional – respected by some, at least – who could rise up over six-feet tall, flash his blue eyes and handsome smile at the jury, and make an impression that led to just verdicts. He was a trustworthy, solid, upstanding man – a substantial presence – and he gave it all to the aid of his clients. He had done so for thirty years in New Orleans where standards were high, expectations were low, and hard-charging lawyers were not in short supply. And where the judges were sterling (though some went to jail).

Experiencing such family and personal threats from the Cubans and feeling the resulting rage grow within him made Tubby think that maybe he needed a new line of work – something more para-military. Staring into the campfire, he tortured himself with thoughts about how he should, how he could, combat such malevolent forces.

"Never screw a client. Never lie to the judge," he said to the

TONY DUNBAR

trees. He had believed that, and done that, for his entire career.
And now?

* * *

Tubby made it one day and one night in his cramped Coleman
tent before he began to get bored and found himself tempted by
a nagging desire to visit an old flame. A year or so ago she had
lived close by to this camp. Creaking to his feet and blowing
some life into last night's bonfire, he fixed up a hearty one-pan
breakfast of scrambled eggs, ashes, and bacon and washed it
down with burned coffee. Blame it on the lonely serenity of his
camp, or all the violence he was sick of in New Orleans, but it
suddenly made good sense to attend to his unfinished business
with Ms. Sylvester. He decided to wash up, shave as best he
could, and take a drive.

He had met Faye back before Katrina while playing in a
church softball league in New Orleans. She was the den mother
for a house full of runaways in Mississippi operated by a sandy-
haired preacher improbably named Rev. Buddy Holly, no relation to the teen idol. Said house was only about twenty miles
from Tubby's camp. Ironically, Tubby's own daughter Debbie
had been one of the kids they took into residence for a brief,
troubled, and strange time in her life. But she had bounced
back, and not long after Rev. Holly had performed the marriage
service for Debbie Dubonnet and Marcos, who had been
together now for almost twelve years. Long story short, Tubby
had gotten to know the bustling house-mom pretty well.

From the first time they met, he had liked Faye, a gangling,
touchingly awkward tall woman with short black hair and a

20

pretty good throw to first. He had liked her a lot. They grew close over the course of several days before she told Tubby the truly stunning news that broke them up – the news was that she had previously been married to Marcus Dementhe, the truly evil District Attorney of Orleans Parish. They were divorced, thank God, but Tubby couldn't even picture this monster with Faye. He had spent months, during his encounters with the "Lucky Man," trying to get Dementhe put into prison for murder, or at least for moral corruption. After her revelation, Faye and Tubby had both withdrawn in embarrassment from their relationship.

A couple of years later, after Katrina, and after her stunning revelation had lost its power, he had sought out Faye again, and they began a long-distance romance. At that point, she lived in a forest cabin, built on land made cheap by the hurricane, and she had begun a job as a guidance counselor in a religious boarding school in Waveland. Once again, the venerable Rev. Holly was involved, this time as the school's headmaster. Unfortunately, their renewed relationship soon became difficult. He couldn't talk Faye into moving to New Orleans, where her bad memories lived, and he didn't see how he could make a living in rural Mississippi. Hell, he'd have to take another bar exam. Not to mention it was next to impossible to find a decent place to eat.

They had had a fight about it one night, and she basically said he didn't have the intestinal fortitude to commit to anyone. Stung by her criticism, he left. That was Tubby's version of it. But yesterday afternoon, floating in the creek, he had to recognize that what she had actually said was that he, himself, was emotionally damaged goods. In any case, she had kicked him

out of her cabin – and her life. The emotional "damage" might
have been true enough, though he blamed that on his own
previous marriage. It had left him with … what? A certain
impermeability to love, divine or human? Or just a tough hide,
some might say.

The things Faye had said had been awfully harsh. Surely he
deserved a little more mercy. This was even more true given his
recent business with the Cubans, the shooting, and the mayhem
in New Orleans. Hell, he might even be a candidate for sym-
pathy. And he was tired of being by himself in his smoky camp.

The plan was to drive over to Faye Sylvester's cabin and
show up unannounced, not always a prudent plan where old
lovers were involved.

CHAPTER 3

Faye Sylvester's little house, nestled in tall turkey pines with a weedy pasture out front, was just as he had remembered it, but there were a lot more flowers everywhere. This was the time for them, after the long autumn and the sudden winter freeze.

He saw a silver Honda Fit SUV parked at the end of her drive with a bumper sticker that read, "Nasty Women for Jesus." There were also two motorcycles on kickstands on the slab under her raised porch.

"Definitely the right place," Tubby said to himself. Dogs were barking.

He got out of his car slowly, wary of animals guarding the environs, and slowly climbed up onto the unpainted wooden porch. All of the barking was coming from inside.

Faye Sylvester answered his knock on the door. She was still quite a looker, in her plaid work shirt and jeans, her hair tied up in a scarf – but the black eyes flashed.

"What the hell are you doing here?" she demanded.

Tubby almost stepped back. "Just wanted to talk," he managed to say. "You haven't changed a bit, Faye." He smiled. She shook her head and let him in. A brown pit bull sniffed at him menacingly.

"I'm practicing with my band," she said, "They're on the back porch. So, what brings you to Mississippi?"

"Band? What do you play?"

"I sing," she told him, leaning back against the stove. "We do hymns. Sort of country rock." She gestured at a small sofa in the pine-paneled living room.

"That sounds terrific," he said. "What about a cup of coffee?" He sat down.

"I'm all out of coffee. Tubby, why did you come?" She remained standing.

"I'd like to talk, that's all. I think there is more that should be said about us."

"No, there's not," she told him, crossing her arms tightly. "You had your chance and you blew it." It was a verdict on so much of what was happening in the lawyer's life at that moment that it hit him hard.

And for just a second he lost it. "Well, I'll be goddamned!" he shouted and got back to his feet. "Here we had this thing…"

"What thing?" a voice asked from behind him. A skinny guy with wire-rimmed spectacles came through the open door. He was at least ten years younger than Tubby, or Faye for that matter, and he was wearing weathered blue jeans and sneakers with no socks.

"Tubby Dubonnet, a guy I used to know. Meet Jack Stolli, boyfriend. Jack's from Hattiesburg." Tubby's jaw dropped.

"I get it," he said, and made his way to the door.

"You know what, Tubby?" Faye advised. "With all of your anger you ought to take up the keyboards or the steel guitar."

He split. It was the most inglorious retreat he had ever endured.

* * *

In the meantime, a certain tennis handsome in New Orleans named Raisin Partlow could see that his young friend, the contortionist, was experiencing hallucinations.

"The desert is too big," she said.

Her name was Jenny. Raisin remembered that much about her. She had a luxurious head of yellow hair that fell in waves of unruly wet curls down below her shoulders.

"It is big, but this is a big city." Raisin murmured. "It's a very nice city, with lots of green trees, and it is very verdant. There is moisture everywhere. No deserts here." He was a little high himself, but on a conventional cocktail. She had shown up at his apartment already launched on some special trip of her own. The contortionist had large blue eyes. She was less than five feet tall.

She looked at him with suspicion.

"It's true," Raisin added. "We have rain all the time and the river keeps rolling on." They were seated at the tiny table in Raisin's tiny kitchen. He had a compact apartment dominated by a bookcase full of literary classics from the last century, many of which he had, in fact, read. There was an original painting by George Dureau by the refrigerator.

"Show me the river," she said.

That sounded like a bad idea. You probably should not take a hallucinating person out to the river, he thought. The Mississippi was extremely mesmerizing and enticing enough even when you were completely straight.

"You'll just have to take my word for that," he said, "but

look out the window. See all the trees? Very green. We are absolutely not in a desert."

"Ah." She abruptly got up from her chair and went to stare out the window. "I see what you mean," she returned to say. An afternoon thunderstorm in New Orleans had turned the day dark as night. Wind gusts made the trees whip around every minute or so and then get still again.

"Is this a hurricane?" she asked.

"No, babe. No hurricanes in the spring. This is just a regular storm. Why not kick back and get a little shut-eye?"

"I saw the moon."

He thought it was probably a streetlight. "You might want to lie down and rest for a few minutes," he suggested. "I can wake you up later." The girl was someone he had met in a wine bar a week before, and with whom he had enjoyed a quick romance. Quirky, but so unusual that she got his full attention. The parts of her body, her fingers for example, moved independently as if belonging to separate creatures. While one hand stroked the stem of her glass the other tapped the table to the music at an entirely different tempo. And her feet did different things. One rested calmly across her knee while the other waved about doing calisthenics under her chair. She also spoke in very poetic but not necessarily cogent sentence fragments. He thought she was gorgeous.

She was a circus performer, he recalled, a sword swallower who could also twist herself into a bread box. They did small parties, she explained, and sometimes latched onto travelling shows. She had trained in Hungary.

And at present she was entirely zonked. He was surprised that she remembered where he lived.

"Will you bring me more drugs?" Jenny asked.

"I beg your pardon. That's not my…"

"Of course not." Jenny suddenly got energized and started doing some back-stretching exercises, which wasn't so easy in the small room. Raisin was beginning to get the picture. Some severe weather event had happened in her psyche. While studying her, he took the opportunity to pour himself another martini.

"Are you sure we are related?" She was bending over backwards till her hands reached the floor. "Wow!" she exhaled, straightening up. "If your dad was Phil and if his brother was my dad Brazos, then I'd say the answer is yes." She took a walk around the room, where there wasn't much to see. He had no idea what she was talking about.

"You're pretty high," he told her. "Normally I might be interested in ravishing your beautiful body, but, sweetheart, you need to come way down."

"I've been way down," she said, twisting to face him. "The son of a bitch took pictures of me when I was down. I know he did it! And he won't give them back!"

"I don't quite get what you're talking about, babe. How about some chai tea, with maybe some honey. Look, I've got some music."

He popped up and keyed in soft mood sounds, no lyrics, almost white noise, the kind that induces sleep.

"Oh, I hate that," she said. "I want to lie in the sand, gray sand, pink sand, black sand, like the Mojave Desert."

"Are you hungry?" he asked. Actually, he had a freezer full of vodka, a refrigerator full of cheese, a wok, and a toaster but no bread, so it was better that she wasn't.

"Don't you get it?" she asked suddenly, her voice rising. "He was making me lovely, but he took pictures. Of all my beautiful fountains. Emotional rape is just as rotten."

"Geez, that's bad. I can call the..." Raisin almost said "cops", but he saw her start to freak out. She jumped up and ran back to look out the window.

"Maybe it's time I took you home," he suggested.

"You got that, dude." She spun around the room like a top.

Raisin had a car. It was a loaner from his most recent love interest who had the good sense to return to New York City to pursue her marital career. She had bequeathed him her bitty Spark to buzz around town in. He now considered it his own.

"Do you want to get rid of me?" she asked, changing her position and kneeling on the rug in front of him.

"No, of course not. You live in the Bywater?"

"Yes, across town." She got up and touched her toes, and repeated it ten times, while he got his jacket and keys.

Raisin had questions about this woman's story. Had a doctor made her beautiful, or had he raped her? What sort of private party hires circus performers? Was this a New Orleans entertainment genre that had somehow escaped his attention? What sort of drugs was she taking? Was she the type who could get violent? How do Hungarians respond to emotional distress? The first thing to do was get her in the car.

Driving through traffic with brake lights abounding, rain squalls about, red lights above, neon signs to the right and left, their disjointed conversation continued.

"It's all aglow," she said. "How was it growing up with my dad? Did he spend some time in the clink?"

28

"Can't tell you," Raisin said, "but I heard he was one beautiful dude."

"What was he in for? Dad was a lawyer." Raisin actually had no knowledge of her dad, but he was almost starting to believe that he was an old friend of the family.

"Just bullshit, I always heard." He looked out the window at the passing scene. There was the Hit and Run Liquor Store. "Doesn't leave much to the imagination," he said to himself.

"What?"

"Nothing." The traffic was backed up at Jackson Avenue.

"Pelicans game tonight," he mentioned.

"I love pelicans," she crooned, leaning back in her seat with her knees near her chin.

The cars ahead cleared enough for Raisin to pilot his microscopic car onto the I-10.

"Dangerous up here," she commented, as trucks whizzed by.

"Not for long." Their exit came up soon. Descending safely into the neighborhood, Raisin patted himself on the back.

"I always heard you were crazy," she told Raisin. *Not as crazy as you*, he thought.

"I am crazy, of course," he admitted. But he doubted that she had ever heard anything about him.

"How did you get that way?" she asked.

He waited for the light go from green to red before he tried to respond to that, but he avoided her question anyway.

Instead of answering, he asked, "So you, are you going to be all right? When we met last week you said something about wanting to leave the country."

"To where?" she interrupted. "To Sweden or Denmark?

The Russians could be there tomorrow. To Canada? How is that different from the United States? To Australia? I can't afford that."

"We're all stuck here. But…"

"But what?" She was intensely concerned and was sitting up straight in her seat.

"But here we are in New Orleans."

"The man has destroyed me," she said.

"The man, the man," Raisin sing-songed.

"The doctor man," she said.

"Is this your place?" he asked.

"No," she said. "How cool is that?" and jumped out of the car.

"Goodnight." Raisin whispered to her disappearing shadow.

* * *

In a rage, or a daze, Tubby piloted his Corvette down the long straight gravel road from Faye Sylvester's cabin, through miles of pulpwood plantations, their masses of green limbs like a tunnel covering the gravel road on its run toward the sea. Destination – the Nazarene Diggers School on the edge of the Gulf of Mexico, and the Reverend Buddy Holly. Tubby had never been there, but Faye had described it as a beautiful place.

Near the beach, a discreet iron sign announced that he had found his school. Its entrance was by a short lane which led to an old mansion erected in sight of the waves gently lapping a low seawall. It was late afternoon, and a few young people lounged about on the spotty grass lawn. They were reading on their laptops or absorbed by their phones and paid him no attention. Inside the doors of the large stone building a sign on a small stand pointed him toward "Administration."

Tubby rapped on the door that said "Office," and Rev. Holly answered. Overcome by his feelings of desperation the past few weeks and his disastrous meeting with Faye, Tubby almost gave the man a hug, but he restrained himself.

"Ah, Mr. Dubonnet," the surprised headmaster said. "It's been so long. How is Debbie, and what beings you to the Nazarene Diggers Academy?"

"I've had some rough patches, Padre," Tubby said. "Do you have a few minutes?"

An exasperated look flitted over Holly's face, but he acquiesced. He showed Tubby into his comfortable office lined with books and children's drawings and sat the lawyer down in a threadbare armchair. Tubby accepted a cup of coffee and explained that he had come to Mississippi for solitude, and, he needed some advice. All right, spiritual advice.

Rev. Holly nodded sympathetically, and for the next hour he got an earful about Tubby's "involvement" in the shooting of a dangerous ex-policeman on a New Orleans levee, topped off with an account of the lawyer's strained relationship with Faye Sylvester.

Holly listened carefully but finally wanted his afternoon wine and decided to cut it short. When the penitent ran out of steam for a moment, the confessor broke in with, "I forgive you for all that, Tubby. You are a man around whom bad things seem to happen, and I'm sure you do your best. Whether the Lord forgives you, however, is between you and Her. Get on your knees!" the preacher commanded.

"Why?"

"It's how you ask for help."

"OK." Tubby acquiesced and carefully got down on the rug.

"Now, we will pray!" Holly told him.

"Why aren't you on your knees?"

"What?"

"Shouldn't you be, too?"

Holly thought about it for a couple of seconds before sighing and kneeling beside Tubby. "Lord, we have a problem here," he began.

Some of the rest of the long prayer went over Tubby's head, but the gist of it was that the fate of his soul wasn't yet one hundred percent determined, and that he had some work to do to straighten himself out with the big gal in the sky.

"Thanks, Buddy," he said when they finally got to "amen" and both stood up.

"Don't you feel better?" the preacher asked.

"Yeah, I guess I do," Tubby admitted.

"Did I hear you say that Faye has a boyfriend?"

"She said so. I met him. A guy named Jack Stolli."

Holly's face darkened. "Every one of us needs to be forgiven for something," he said. "Every one of us is weak."

"Sure, I know that," Tubby agreed as they said their goodbyes. But he didn't really believe it. What an interesting experience that had been. It took him back to his adolescence at First Baptist in Bunkie, Louisiana, where prayer was a daily event.

But did he feel forgiven?

* * *

He was still thinking about this same question the next day as he once again floated in circles on the creek. Tubby wasn't sure whether he would fare better with a male or a female God. But there was one thing Rev. Holly had been quite definite about, Tubby recalled. He had to make amends. He must apologize to Faye for his boorish behavior and wish her well in her new relationship. And he needed to have a conversation with the New Orleans cops.

So that's what he determined to do.

CHAPTER 4

Back in Louisiana it was nearly midnight. The stretch of St. Bernard Highway by the Chalmette Refinery was empty of traffic so Ednan Amineh made the mistake of punching the gas. Unluckily, just as he passed the parish "ruins," the last of this locale's historic planation homes, which had now collapsed into a small heap of stones in the overgrown median separating the lanes of the highway, the terrible flashing blues lit up his rear-view mirror.

"Jeez, Louise!" Ednan exclaimed. He had always been un-lucky.

The first thing the troopers noticed, while they were watching the suspect searching for wallet and driver's license, was that there was a neat round hole with a spider web of cracks around it in the passenger side of the front windshield.

"Hey, Ned." The cop on that side put his pinkie finger into the hole and wiggled it around. His face popped from blue to black as his car lights rotated.

"How'd you get that, sir?" Ned, the policeman at the driver's window, asked. He peered down at his newly interesting sus-pect. "Looks sort of like a bullet hole."

"I don't know a thing about it," Ednan said. "It didn't use to be there."

"Is that a fact?" Ned commented. "Well, I need you to get out of your vehicle. Very slowly."

Ednan did as he was told and found himself forced face-down onto the hood and spread out nice and wide for a pat down.

"You got the registration for this car?" the cop asked him. Ednan's chin and left cheek hugged the smooth warm metal.

"It's in the glove?" he suggested hopefully.

"We'll see about that." The officer rested his hand firmly on the small of Ednan's back, keeping him in place, while his partner, a young guy whom Ednan thought he recognized from high school, began rummaging through the car.

An automobile passed and honked. Probably somebody he knew. Pretty soon news of this would be all over Chalmette. The detainee could hear a ship's horn on the river, and the noises of a garbage truck nearby crushing its load. These were comforting sounds somehow. This town of Chalmette, adjacent to New Orleans, was his home.

"Is this your knife?" asked the young cop, dangling in front of the detainee's nose a blade with a mass of duct tape wrapped around its handle.

"No sir," Ednan said. "Never saw it before."

"Is this your car?" the policeman inquired, still polite.

"Not exactly," Ednan admitted.

"Who does it belong to?"

"I'm not sure," he replied forlornly. This was all going to be bad.

"Sir, we're going to need you to sit in the back of our patrol car while we sort this out." Suddenly he was cuffed and pulled upright.

"I was just in the wrong place at the wrong time," Ednan protested.

"Roger that," the young cop said tonelessly. They pulled their suspect into the police car and left him to reflect upon his situation while they got busy on their radio.

And the news was not good. It seems that two deceased Vietnamese, deceased with several bullet holes and possibly knife wounds, had been recently discovered in the West End neighborhood of New Orleans, not far from the yacht harbor. A witness had reported a dark-complected man in a car. Ednan touched both of those bases.

Before he knew it, Ednan was being driven to the St. Bernard Parish line in Arabi to be turned over to the city cops.

"Wrong place and wrong time," the young man moaned over and over to himself.

CHAPTER 5

In the morning while Ednan was getting his bail set, Tubby Dubonnet dutifully drove slowly back down the washboard gravel road through the pulpwood forests toward Faye Sylvester's house. He was mulling over how he should apologize and having a hard time of it. She was entitled to her own life, and he was to his, but he had sort of thought that she would be happy to see him and would at least give him the courtesy of a heart-to-heart talk about where their relationship had soured and whether it could be saved, on a friendly basis only of course. But obviously it was not to be.

He wasn't paying much attention to the road behind him, or in front, for that matter, since he hadn't seen anything but trees and cow pastures for the past fifteen miles, but a dirt trail into the woods appeared to the side and provided the opportunity for Tubby to pull over and compose himself. And to reflect upon how he hoped this conversation was going to go.

Just as he pulled off, he was nearly blown into the yellow-clay ditch by something that must have been a big pick-up truck blazing at top speed. It went past in a roar, scattering gravel, and disappeared in a cloud of dust.

Tubby parked in the thicket and rehearsed.

"Faye, don't shoot," his conversation might begin. "I'm just here to say I'm sorry."

He didn't get very far with his imaginary conversation, and after ten minutes of internal dialogue he got his car rolling again.

At the cabin, a white car was there, which Tubby now figured must belong to the boyfriend. What was his name? Jerk Off? Something like that.

The dogs were barking when he hit the porch, but nobody came to answer the bell, which was in fact a cow bell hung from a string of glass beads. He knocked on the door, and it opened a crack. Tubby took the chance and poked his head inside to call, "Anybody home?"

Somebody was. Faye was lying face down on her living room rug with her chest in a pool of blood. Her pit bull was dancing around in circles, yapping hysterically.

He ignored both the revulsion in his chest and the frightened dog and knelt beside her. She was warm. He took her shoulder and hip and turned her over. Her face was angry. Her throat had been cut and the blood was just starting to dry.

Tubby abruptly stood up and dug into his pocket for his phone. He called 911.

After the call and while he waited for somebody to show up, the lawyer walked back to the kitchen and found the boyfriend dead on the floor. "Got him with a knife, too," Tubby said out loud and decided he would wait outside.

Leaning for support against the porch rail he uttered an angry, intense, and tearful prayer, to whom he couldn't say.

A mockingbird, pretending to be a blue jay, sang high in a tall pine tree. The morning breeze blew sweetly.

CHAPTER 6

Somehow, E.J. Chaisson got his French Quarter lease done without Tubby's input, and he got the Prince and his people successfully settled into the three-story house with galleries on Dauphine Street. They plunked down the deposit and their first three months' rent in cash. Nice crisp Ben Franklins, bills so new they stuck together. E.J. could barely restrain himself from grabbing the exalted figure and embracing him.

After a most cordial parting, Chaisson sped out to the Fairgrounds in his red Cadillac to test his luck with the horses. He got there in time to bet on the ninth race. He lost that one, but didn't much care. He had been trying for two years to find a tenant for his beautifully-restored old mansion, and finally he had scored. Big time.

Prince Bazaar was E.J.'s new main man, and their conversation, as the money was nonchalantly transferred from one supple leather pouch to another, centered on how the Prince could throw a memorable party, one that would make an enormous impression upon the social leaders of New Orleans.

E.J. was a good person to ask about this, since he had been tracking the mysteries of New Orleans society and pursuing the same goal of acceptance for his entire life. The Prince wanted to meet "fun people, young people." OK, that eliminated the true social core, the old established set. You could have a good enough time at the Metairie or New Orleans Country Clubs, but not exactly "fun." Especially not if the hosts were the oddly-dressed characters who made up the Sultan's crew. These venues had already been grabbed for Mardi Gras balls and events anyway. One just can't throw a party and expect to enter the mystic world of Carnival. It takes years – years – generations, even, as E.J. well knew – to gain admission to better society. A Deb party? No, the Prince had no available college juniors, and it was way too late in the season anyhow.

"I've got it, Your Highness! We'll throw a charity ball!"

"That sounds fine. But for what charity? What would be good, do you think?"

"Homeless kids and crime fighting are always the best," E.J. counseled, "but if you want people to be in a happy frame of mind, I'd suggest the arts."

"Arts would be fine." The Prince nodded jovially, as if telling himself a private joke.

"Of course, people expect an open bar for a really nice event, and I'm still not sure if booze, you know, lines up with your beliefs."

"Whether or not it does," the Prince said solemnly, "we can make accommodations. But, please, no art that insults God. Or the Pope," he added.

"Hey, that may be a challenge, but we can manage it," E.J. assured him. "Let me get to work. I want your stay here to be just as you desire it to be in every single detail."

"That is wonderful, and in our invitation let's call me the 'Sultan'."

"Even better than 'Prince'," E.J. gushed.

At the track, where E.J. always did his best thinking, he came up with the name of Peggy O'Flarity. She was, he believed, Tubby Dubonnet's most recent dating interest, and she was also plugged into all sorts of arts organizations. He would call her as soon as he placed his bets, and she'd give him the low-down.

CHAPTER 7

During the half an hour that Tubby waited at Faye's cabin for the law to arrive, he thought about many things. His memories of Faye Sylvester, when she was alive and responded to his touch, were the most vivid of those things.

He tried to make those images go away. There was the jasmine in the Mississippi air to think about, for instance, and the quietness of the woods, where the faint hum of distant trucks was overcome by the lazy buzzing of insects and the rustling of the trees when gusts of wind made their tall tops sway.

He also thought about various crime scenes he had been to and the surprising and usually suppressed images of dead bodies he had seen. The less recent corpses were better, he thought bitterly. The ones whose blood had already clotted. The ones too far gone to help or envision as almost alive. The ones unlike Faye Sylvester and that man inside on the kitchen floor. He wished the police would hurry up.

It was so quiet you could hear a mouse pee on cotton, the old expression came to mind, but it didn't stay that way long.

The flashing lights finally came through the trees, bouncing over the ruts in the winding driveway. Tubby was sitting in one of the rocking chairs on the porch, but he stood up to face the officer who got out of the first vehicle on whose door "Sheriff of Pearl River County" was stenciled. He was a big man, maybe six-four, bigger than Tubby, and he had a "hat just like a Mountie."

The presumed sheriff spat into the scrubgrass yard and marched up to the porch to see what the call was all about. Another sheriff's car crunched down the drive, and two men in similar gray uniforms hopped out.

"Tubby Dubonnet," Tubby said, extending his hand. The other big man took it and said he was Sheriff Brady Stockstill.

"Are you the one who called?" he asked.

"Yeah," Tubby said. "There's two of them dead inside."

The sheriff cocked an eyebrow at the lawyer.

"I didn't do it," Tubby said. "I just found them and called you."

The sheriff motioned his men forward and indicated that one should keep an eye on Dubonnet. He entered the front door with the other. A third police car arrived, and two more men in uniform got out and came to the porch, hands on their holstered weapons, staring hard at the stranger, the attorney.

The Sheriff came back outside. "Two dead," he said. "One of them's that teacher down at the church school. Call Doctor James, Darryl. We're going to be here for a while. Why don't you have a seat here, Mister... What did you say your name was?"

"Tubby Dubonnet. I'm a lawyer from New Orleans."

"Is that right? Lawyers are my favorite people. Branscomb, pat him down for me, would you?"

Tubby allowed himself to be felt all over. Branscomb showed

palms-up to the Sheriff. Nothing there but a wallet, which he handed to his boss.

The Sheriff looked at it and stuffed it into his shirt pocket, right under his star. He settled heavily into one of the rocking chairs and gestured for Tubby to reclaim his seat in the other.

"So," he said, rubbing his face with his hands, "tell me why you are here in Pearl River County."

In this comfortable manner Tubby was interrogated on the porch for quite some time. A doctor arrived, as did an ambulance, and soon the Sylvester yard was full of vehicles and official cars parked all the way to the main road. The lawyer explained things as best he could, keeping it simple as was his training and inclination.

At one point, he mentioned that a New Orleans judge would vouch for his good character, and he was allowed to make a call to verify that. He dialed up Judge Alvin Hughes, who had been a classmate in law school and a long-time friend, but unfortunately the Judge was on the bench. Tubby left a message with the clerk.

He thought another reference, from one Adrian Duplessis, now the Sheriff of Orleans Parish, might be good, and Sheriff Stockstill let him make that call, too. Here Tubby had a little more luck, and got Adrian, whom he had long represented as Monster Mudbug, theatrical float-builder and Mardi Gras extravaganza.

Tubby explained his situation to the new Sheriff Duplessis in a very condensed form.

"Sure, let me talk to him," Adrian quickly said.

Tubby handed his phone to Sheriff Stockstill. Listening to one end of the conversation he heard:

"Yeah."

"Yeah."

"Yeah. He wants to talk to you." Stockstill passed the phone back to Tubby.

"Yes, Adrian," the lawyer said hopefully.

"I told him you've been a good attorney for a long time. Ain't that the truth? Now listen, when you get back to town, I got a guy in here needs to see a lawyer real bad. I'm taking a special interest in him because I know him from growing up. He's not a bad guy, just stupid, you know what I mean?"

"Absolutely."

"Okay, when you get out of your Mississippi deal, please come see me."

"Right. Okay."

They hung up.

"Okay?" Tubby asked.

"Okay. So you're a legit citizen," Sheriff Stockstill conceded. "What I'm going to do is have Branscomb here," he indicated his deputy who stared at Tubby as if he were a venomous lizard, "get all of your pertinent information, but we're going to let you go on about your business."

"Thanks," Tubby said.

The Sheriff nodded. "It's also important to me," he said, looking carefully at Tubby, "that they were killed with a sharp instrument, and you don't have one on you. Of course, you could have thrown it into the trees." He swept his arm towards the woods. But you don't really seem to be the type. You're more of a boxer, aren't you?"

"I was a wrestler in college," Tubby said. "But the main thing is, Faye and I were friends."

"Sure. That's what you said. Don't worry. We'll find out who did it. We always do." He handed Tubby back his wallet, gave him a handshake designed to crush small bones, and stood up to take a long, deep breath. Without another word he went back inside the house.

The reference to "a sharp object" conjured up an image of Tubby's recent client, Angelo Spooner, who had wrongly been thought by some to be an axe murderer.

Branscomb got all of Tubby's particulars down to his shoe size and let him go.

The lawyer walked slowly to his car, navigating a tight passage past several parked police vehicles, reached the blacktop, and floored it.

CHAPTER 8

The next morning, after spending a fitful night in his own bed in New Orleans, Tubby showed up at his office. He was early and arrived before his secretary Cherrylynn. She had, however, left a neatly-stacked pile of messages on his desk, and among these was a note to call E.J. Chaisson with the comment, "Needs A Lease. Paying Job, He Says." Though he found it intriguing, Tubby had bigger fish to fry.

Today he planned to have his conversation with the cops. It would be unkind to the dignity of the law were he to continue on the well-worn path of his legal practice while concealing the evidence he knew of the crime of murdering Detective Kronke at the conclusion of the "Fat Man" investigation. He imagined how he would defend the killer. He would emphasize the mental stress he had been under at the time and, more than that, there was the justifiability of the homicide. Detective Paul Kronke had to be stopped before he killed someone else. As everyone knows, a justifiable homicide is no murder at all. But he didn't expect to get the chance to defend this case in court.

The first step was to locate Lieutenant Adam Mathewson, who had been a witness to Kronke's shooting on the levee and who had very nearly been another one of the victims.

Tubby was surprised to be informed by the woman who answered the phone at police headquarters that Detective Mathewson, like Kronke before his sudden death, had also retired. No, she would not take a message, but, since Tubby claimed to be Adam's old friend from St. Agapius parochial school, she suggested, "You might try Priebus's bar." Further research revealed that this was "Priebus's Trumpet Lounge" on Roman Street near St. Claude.

That's where Tubby found the former policeman at six o'clock that same evening. As he walked the block from his car to the outwardly decrepit dive, Tubby spied the detective's burly shoulders departing the bar and lumbering away on the sidewalk. He hurried ahead to catch him.

"Wait, Adam," the lawyer called.

Mathewson took one quick look over his shoulder and ducked between two parked vehicles. He came up with a gun pointed over the hood directly at Tubby's midsection.

"Yo, Hey!" Tubby protested, coming up short. "What's up, partner? Just want to talk."

"Stay where you are, dude. What do you want with me?" Mathewson's voice was like a truck grinding gears. His face was flushed and ringed with stubbly whiskers.

"I want to talk to you, that's all. You were there, right? You saw the whole thing!"

"You've got to be kidding me," Mathewson said. "Don't you take a step forward! The man is wasted a foot from me, and *now* you want to talk? Bullshit!"

"That's just it!" Tubby yelled. "I want all of the facts to be known!"

"I'm retired, you donkey. Get the hell out of here before I blow off your knees!"

"Now look here," Tubby began, taking a step forward, "My intentions..."

In a flash, Mathewson was gone. He bolted into the dark street and ran away into the shadows.

Boy, he's fast for a big dude, Tubby thought to himself.

Evidently, Lt. Adam Mathewson was not going to serve his purpose.

Back in his own car, Tubby worked the phone. He learned that the detective in charge of investigating the death of Paul Kronke was Sgt. Johnny Vodka. Tubby had met this Latino cop years before in his search for the elusive "Crime Czar" and had the impression that he was an intense and honest man.

In time, he got Vodka on the phone, but the best that could be arranged was coffee the next morning at the Trolley Stop on St. Charles Avenue. Tubby was forced to spend another night home alone with his memories and conscience.

Tubby realized that he was in a weird mental place. Shootings happened all the time. Kronke was already yesterday's news, and it was affecting him more than it was anyone else. But the slate had to be wiped, didn't it? The music had to be faced.

In the meantime, he stayed away from places that to him were pleasurable, like Janie's Monkey Business Bar. He didn't call his girlfriend Peggy O'Flarity either, being not ready yet to let her know he was back in town. But because he needed some contact, he did call his daughters, Christine, Debbie and Collette, each in turn according to youngest first.

Collette, who was a recent LSU at Lafayette grad and was

dating a rap musician, had all of her shields up. Some kind of electronic music provided the background for, "Leave a message when you hear the drums."

"It's me. Just called to say hi," he told her phone.

Christine answered her phone, but she was on the run to study, she said, at some friends' house. She was in grad school.

"Where have you been, Daddy?" she asked in a rush.

"Over in Mississippi, uh…" he said.

"Did you have a good trip?"

"I made it back" was all he could come up with. "How's school?"

"Great. Listen, can I call you back? I'm getting in the car now, and I'm late."

Debbie, the only one of his daughters with a child, was now in her early thirties. She was actually willing to talk, though he had caught her at work. She was in the music business, as in selling pools of song rights owned by undiscovered local Swamp Pop artists to investor funds. Tubby was a little in awe of this career, which seemed to be lucrative though he didn't understand it. He told Debbie that he had visited Rev. Buddy Holly in Mississippi, which was exciting to her since Holly had officiated at Debbie's marriage to Marcos a few years back.

"And do you remember meeting Faye Sylvester?" he asked her. "You know, at Buddy's farm?"

"Of course," Debbie said. "She's a beautiful lady. She got me to talk about a lot of things that really troubled me back then. How is she doing?"

"Well, the sad thing is, she's passed away," Tubby told her.

"Oh no!" Debbie exclaimed. "Was she sick?"

"I don't know all the details," her father hedged, "but I expect I will go to her funeral."

"Didn't you and she have, sort of, an affair?"

"Where'd you get that?"

"I know lots of things."

"Yeah, I guess we did," Tubby told her. "But it ended."

"Will you let me know when the service is?"

"Yes."

"Are you okay, Daddy?"

"I'll be fine."

* * *

At night it was really creepy in Central Lockup. The televisions, which had been running endless music videos on Black Entertainment Television all day, were now tuned to reality shows, like "The Real Housewives of Atlanta". Whooping and hollering was discouraged by the constabulary, but the men could still make loud and insulting comments about all of the women who appeared on screen. The TVs were interspersed around the room, but they were all on the same channel. Spirits high, the prisoners could taunt and threaten each other across the bunks. There were fifty beds in the unit, and fifty apiece in three other identical units on the floor. There was a guard station in each unit, but the guard on duty was typically entranced by his or her phone.

Ednan had a cot more or less in the middle of the hall next to Peanut, who was some kind of albino. No one befriended the "Terrorist," as they referred to Ednan, because he could not easily be classified as black, white, or Hispanic. The albino Peanut was another outcast. The two odd prisoners tried to look after each other. Peanut was awaiting trial for breaking into cars, a lot of cars. He had exhausted his neighbors' patience in the Seventh Ward, and somebody snitched him out. But he never hurt anybody, and he never really found anything of value to steal. There was also some male prostitution charge on him, but Ednan didn't believe that one could be true. Peanut would do all right on the outside if only he had a few friends and a chance to get a job, or at least this was to be Ednan's argument as to why some lawyer should help him, if only he had a lawyer. Otherwise he'd be completely screwed since the public defender would probably meet with him only once, the morning of trial, and urge him to take a plea for a year or two in prison. As it was, Peanut was facing two to five.

There was a big dude who liked to walk over to Ednan's spot in the evening and harass him. "Hey, Terrorist," the guy said. "You killed all them Vietnamese people, huh? Was it a hate crime, or what? You just hate slanty-eyed people, or do you hate black people, too?"

"He didn't do that crime, man, and he don't hate black people neither," Peanut said in Ednan's defense. "Him and me are friends, aren't we?"

"You ain't black, Peanut," the man laughed. "You're just some kind of freak."

"I like freaks," Ednan rose up and said. "I don't like anybody but freaks."

"So, I guess that means you don't like me."

"You're all right. When you mind your own business."

"My business is on the outside, Terrorist, and I'll be seeing you when we get out there. You and your cute little man-bun."

Ednan settled back. He fingered his hair, then turned over and closed his eyes. This jail was a creepy place at night.

Ednan had one nice thing to think about. He had a girlfriend named Ayana. They weren't exactly going steady, but Ednan was sure they would be soon, just as quickly as he could get out of this joint.

* * *

Ayana was fair and saucy. She had a very high opinion of herself. She wore nice clothes, since her father had a steady job and doted on her. She was a majorette in her high school marching band and got to shimmy and shake in a tight red-sequined leotard right in front of the horn section. All the boys were so crazy for her they could barely keep time. She wasn't Honor Roll by any means, but she was going to graduate and do well. That was the plan.

She was sorry to hear that Ednan had been arrested. "He's such a sweet dummy," she told her father, but she didn't plan on going to visit him in jail. There was a fine young man named "Stroker" who lived in the neighborhood and who DJ'ed all the local parties. He had a non-stop patter everybody loved and could get you dancing as soon as he flipped on his mike. And he had started to pay attention to Ayana, calling her name when she passed the stoop he hung out on, saying her clothes looked so good, asking when she would go out with him. "Ayana," he sang, "take me to Nirvana." It wasn't going to take much for her to say yes.

In his cot, Ednan fell asleep thinking about Ayana. She stayed awake in her bed at home thinking about Stroker.

CHAPTER 9

"I woke up early this morning. I dreamed about what you did to me!" Jenny, the physique artist, was walking down Magazine Street talking on her phone. "You bastard!" she cried.

"Yeah, you did too!" She continued her monologue. "You took off my panties and you felt me all over. While you had me doped up." She was passing a bakery and people eating croissants at a sidewalk table heard some of this but ignored her. You heard snippets of private conversations all the time these days, and it was okay as long as the people kept moving and didn't burden you with their whole life stories.

"No, you fucking asshole, I don't want to see you again! And I don't want to pay your fucking bill either! And I want my pictures back!"

Around the corner from Valence Street came a band of Mardi Gras Indians marching to loud tambourines and tom-toms. They were chanting in time while pirouetting to display their flaming plumage and costumes. A small but spirited second line had formed up behind them. Most of the people were jazzed up and dancing and drinking plastic cups of beer.

"I can't hear you!" the woman screamed into the phone. She was so stressed that she started to exercise her shoulders back and forth, limbering herself up to squeeze into some tiny safe space.

The parade turned at the corner, in the direction she was headed. She held back on the sidewalk, waiting for them to pass.

"What, you asshole? I can't hear you!" she yelled again.

She stared helplessly at her dead phone and slumped against the wall of a pizza restaurant. She punched in the number of her gymnast girlfriend, who answered and got a teary earful.

"I just wanted to be shaped and sculpted," Jenny sobbed. And it was true. It took a nip and a tuck sometimes to keep the body so small. Where she got the idea that the doctor took pictures, however, was less clear. Someone might have told her, or it might have come to her in a dream, but that did not matter. Jenny was convinced it was true.

"I'm going to get him!" she assured her friend. "We'll bring him out to the forest where all the birds can see and finish him there."

Her friend caught the "we" but did not object. She got her personal kicks going, with Jenny, where no man had gone before.

* * *

Tubby got to the restaurant early, but he found Officer Vodka already seated at a square table packing away his eggs, biscuits, and bacon. There were crumbs on the floor. He waved Tubby over, while at the same time talking to someone on the blue-tooth stuck behind his ear.

"Fuck no," Vodka told somebody.

Tubby took a seat.

"Fuck no!" Vodka said again, louder, and twirled his eyes apologetically at the lawyer.

The waitress passed by and Tubby ordered coffee and a menu, but he really wasn't hungry. He had his toothbrush and a change of clothes in the car, ready to go to jail.

The coffee came while Vodka was still on the phone, but he finally said, "Later," to the somebody and asked Tubby, "What's up?" He grabbed his own mug and took a gulp.

"I don't know if you remember me, but we met..."

"Sure. Couple of years back. Before the storm. You're a lawyer. I remember who you are. You were after our nutcase district attorney, Marcus Dementhe. What about it?"

Vodka was a compact man with curly black hair and a tanned complexion that could have been Italian or Creole, but he was actually Mexican. Tubby noticed that the detective's mouth always moved, whether he was eating, talking, or listening, like he was chewing gum. Tubby guessed him to be about forty years old. The kind of guy who pressed three hundred pounds and ran marathons.

"I understand that you are working the homicide of Paul Kronke, the retired cop who was shot a couple of months ago out by the levee near Magazine Street."

"Yep, that's my crime." Vodka's jaws worked overtime. "It ain't going nowhere. Whatcha got?"

"I have a suggestion about who the perp was."

"Yeah?" Vodka liked that. His eyes lit up. He grabbed a biscuit and stuffed a piece of it in his mouth. "It was a black female. Who was she?"

"What!"

"A black female. There was a reliable witness, whose name is

Lt. Adam Mathewson, and I stress the 'Lieutenant' because he was a highly regarded police officer, and he said, in no uncertain terms, that the shooter was an African-American female."

"Not a white male? Why would he say that?"

"Got me. Because it's true? Because Kronke left behind a whole list of complaints from African-American females who said he had fucked them over? I don't know? What the hell can you tell me about this? I'm all ears."

"Well, that's news to me."

"So, who was she?"

"I really don't know. I guess I have to think about what you are saying."

The waitress came and refilled Tubby's coffee cup.

Vodka was still staring at him. "Want some cream?" he asked Tubby.

"No, I drink it black."

"I don't care for it without cream," Vodka said, his jaw flexing. "You going to eat?"

"No, I'm not too hungry, but this is on me. Have whatever you want. You're my guest. I remember when you nailed Marcus Dementhe. He was one bad dude."

"Thanks, but we didn't nail our cracked D.A. He ran away. He had some kind of fake passport and off he went. Out of the jurisdiction."

That was astonishing news. Faye's deviant ex-husband, who preyed on innocent prostitutes, had slipped the noose.

"When was that?" Tubby asked, fearing his consternation was evident. He absently took one of Vodka's biscuits and started to butter it.

"That was a long time ago, wasn't it, Mr. Dubonnet? It was

like, around the time of Katrina, right? A lot has happened since then. Anyway, Dementhe was just a possible suspect. For a murder, okay, but just a suspect. I don't think there's even a warrant still out for him."

"Where could he have gone?" Tubby couldn't believe he had been too absorbed in lesser matters to notice that Marcus Dementhe was never prosecuted. Maybe the guy would come back to New Orleans and go gunning for Tubby again.

Vodka shrugged. "Where do they welcome criminals? Where is off the grid? I don't know. Bolivia? Venezuela? Ecuador?"

Tubby's mind was in a whirl. Now there was also an ex-husband who really might have wanted Faye Sylvester to suffer.

Vodka broke in. "Anyway, ancient history," he said.

Tubby forgot what he was doing, and his butter knife dropped to the floor.

"Careful, buddy," Vodka cautioned and picked up Tubby's utensil. "So, what's troubling you, man?" the cop asked. "Aren't we catching enough gangsters to suit you? You want us to waste our time chasing after people who didn't do anything."

"Maybe I will take some cream," Tubby said. Vodka handed over the little pitcher, and Tubby stirred some in. "A hell of a way to start the day," he said, to anyone who was listening.

"Sir," Vodka told him abruptly, standing up and tossing his napkin on the table. "Stop wasting my time. I've got too many other crimes to worry about. Let me know if you come up with something real. I've got work to do." Almost as an aside, he mumbled to himself, "This is a sick city."

He was gone.

The waitress returned, and Tubby ordered everything he could think of. He got the Southern Special, with sausage,

TONY DUNBAR

bacon, grits and gravy, and three eggs sunny side up. And an "everything" bagel, heated up, with Philadelphia cream cheese.

"Man." He had to chuckle when she walked away with his order. "It's hard to turn yourself in. I guess maybe I should just practice law."

Waiting for his breakfast to come, he imagined that he was still floating in the creek. His inflated black tube turned him slowly in the sunshine.

The food came, but he ignored it. Deep in his thoughts, big trucks sped past him on the Interstate. They were all going to New Orleans and, if not there, on to Texas, where life's vistas spread out forever. Feeling spacey, he paid for his breakfast and left it on the table.

On his way home, he called Peggy O'Flarity from the car.

"Howdy, stranger," she said. "How have you been?"

"That's a big question," he replied. "What would you think about having dinner tonight?"

"I'm in Nashville, hon. Can't do it."

"Visiting your son?"

"Yes."

"How is he?"

"He's doing okay for being a grad student with a two-year-old baby and a nutty wife. But there's a party Saturday night in New Orleans I think you'll enjoy. Maybe you can take me."

"A party? I don't know. I've been having a difficult couple of weeks."

"Oh, that's too bad. I thought you might be having a bit of a vacation."

"It didn't turn out that way."

"So sorry. I'll call you when I get back, which should be day after tomorrow, and see if I can talk you into having a little fun."

He remembered to check his messages as he drove up Freret Street. One was from Judge Hughes, who basically said he was retiring and on his way out of the world of responsibility. He advised Tubby to cultivate younger friends. What had happened to Mrs. Hughes, Tubby wondered? Did she ever get Hurricane Katrina out of her mind and return from the Bahamas? Maybe that's where Tubby should go. Maybe he had atoned enough. If so, the process wasn't terribly demanding.

Nevertheless he had given atonement a shot, so to speak. He had offered himself to the police. Time to put this entire episode out of mind and get back to the present, where there were certainly problems enough.

CHAPTER 10

There is an Indian tribe nestled in the Ninth Ward, named the Tennessee Street Social Aid & Benevolent Association, organized 1959. It had originally been founded, some say, back in slavery times. Some say it was for runaways and their swamp-dwelling Choctaw protectors, but none of that history got written down. They were a gang, but not a plain and simple gang. They had a turf, but nobody else much wanted it anymore, at least not for the Indians' purposes. The tribe didn't want to control the local drug trade. They just wanted to look pretty.

For that, the members had to make a resplendent garb of headdresses and aprons, patches and umbrellas, to make a man's form bigger, built of a thousand feathers and a million colorful beads. All wholesaled from China, but carefully stitched together by each member, upholding their family traditions. The appearance of the gang on the street – any street – displayed in their dazzling colors was an occasion to sing, dance, and drink, so they were always in demand.

The chief and the two second chiefs of the Tennessee Street Association were discussing business over beer in a grocery and po-boy shop on Dumaine Street. Nobody was wearing their feathers. They had all just come from work.

An important position in the gang had come open – that of
Flag Boy. This was a key job, common to all of the Mardi Gras
Indian groups scattered around New Orleans. During the parade,
the Spy Boy ventured far in advance and sent signals regarding
the whereabouts of adversary gangs and any police back to the
Flag Boy, whose role was to relay those messages to the Chief by
means of his feathery flag on a tall staff. The Tennessee's Flag
Boy had been hit by a city bus and was under semi-permanent
chiropractic care. He was required by his lawyer to stay in bed
until his lawsuit was resolved. Above all, he was under strict
attorney's orders to give up parading, and all other displays of
vigor and mobility, for the duration of the litigation.

"I think my boy Ednan can do it," said the chief.

"He's in jail though, brother," his second pointed out, tapping a Marlboro out of his pack. He couldn't smoke on the job,
so this was pure heaven.

"That's true. He's got to get past that. But he's one of the
gang and understands all the rules and traditions. He was working on a very fine patch for his chest when he got popped."

"He's actually sewing?" The deputy was dubious.

"Yeah. Of course, my wife is helping him. But he's trying
and getting better."

"What about that boy Stroker? You remember his father?"

They all nodded. Stroker's father had been a passionate and
popular man in the neighborhood. But then the chief added, "I
don't know if that was his actual father or not." Everybody
smiled and sipped.

"Anyway, Stroker's never done a lick of work in his life. He
just plays music and struts around the clubs."

"The people like him though," the other second chief said

sagely. "We could use some new blood. Hasn't your daughter Ayana been seeing him?"

"No way, not ever!" the chief shouted. "Don't let me hear that kind of talk! Ayana's got higher goals than some Stroker!"

"All right, all right," his friend said to cool him down. "But we might dig up some parading suit from last year and give the boy a try if Ednan is still in jail when Super Sunday rolls around."

"That would just be embarrassing," the chief said. "Stroker doesn't even know who we really are."

The guys just shrugged, and the conversation shifted to the price of tiny imported glass beads.

CHAPTER 11

Ednan had had a rough few nights in the Orleans Parish Prison. Though the facility was brand spanking new, it had already been found to be unconstitutional and was under Federal court supervision. The main problem, from where Ednan sat on his metal cot, was that the place was full of maniacs who wanted sex and money. And there weren't very many guards. And the ones who showed up for work also seemed to want sex and money.

The other problem was that he was being held on suspicion of murdering some Vietnamese guys, two of them, and he had never even heard of them. He understood that he was going to be taken to court for arraignment that morning when a rotund officer in black informed him he had an attorney visit.

Heart full of hope, the prisoner was escorted to the visiting room, where he found himself seated across from a tall stocky man in a three-piece suit and a head of blond hair, separated from him by a pane of heavy glass. This man gestured at the phone on Ednan's side of the table and the prisoner snatched it up.

"My name is Tubby Dubonnet," the visitor began. "I'm a lawyer. I've been asked to look into your case."

"Praise God for that." Ednan nodded eagerly. "Who called you?"

"Actually, Sheriff Duplessis asked me to speak with you. He says he knows you…"

"Oh, bless you, Monster Mudbug!" Ednan cried, referencing the sheriff's former parade persona. "You are the man!" He pounded the stainless steel table.

"Well, he says he knows you."

"Sure, from forever! We were next-door neighbors on West Casa Calvo Street. His daddy and mine played the horses together. Why I've known Adrian since…"

"Yeah," Tubby interrupted him, "so now you are in a jam for murdering the two Vietnamese kids who got killed over in Lakeview. What's the story?" Tubby opened his palms awaiting an explanation.

"Are you here to be my lawyer?"

"I haven't decided yet. You might do better with a public defender anyway. They know the judges."

"They don't do nothin'." Ednan was sure about that. Everybody in the joint said so.

"Have you got the money to hire a lawyer?"

"Not a whole lot. I've been on some hard times, mister." Ednan wiped his brow, then put his shoulders back. "But I'm good for it. I always pay my bills."

Tubby sighed. He stared at the stalwart and honest Black Sea face. Finally he said, "Let me hear your story, then we'll talk about the particulars."

Ednan had quite a tale to tell, and he blurted it out in one ten-minute monologue.

Turns out, he actually had an alibi. At the very time the two

Vietnamese were killed, Ednan was engaged in stealing a car, exactly the same car in which he had been apprehended, from the parking lot in front of a Discount Zone on Bullard Avenue in New Orleans East. The store was operated by his cousin.

"There was a camera in the lot, I'm pretty sure of that, cause that's what I was told by the guy who was robbing the 7-11."

"Are you saying that the store was being held up while you were stealing a car outside?"

"Yep. It sure was." Ednan's head bobbed up and down.

"And you know the guy who was robbing the store?"

"Not before, no. But he's here in jail, and we talked about it."

"He's in jail, here with you?"

"Right."

Tubby was dubious but said, "Okay."

"True. So his name is Jockey, and he sees me stealing his getaway car, which he had also stolen, but I didn't know that, and he tries to shoot me."

"Tries?"

"Well, he does shoot at me. But he didn't hit me. He put a bullet through the windshield when I was backing out of the parking lot. And, man, I was scorching tires."

"Why did you steal the car?"

"I needed to get back to my aunt's house in Chalmette."

"Why? It was a special occasion?"

"Right, her godchild's christening. I was supposed to be there. So I grabbed the car."

The lawyer considered this. "That's not too bad," he said.

* * *

Tubby had some luck and located the correct assistant district attorney, a young woman named Bianca Maricopa, who it turned out went to school with Tubby's middle daughter Christine. They had both been cheerleaders in high school, though Bianca was a year ahead of Tubby's own.

"Do you remember me?" she asked.

"You betcha," Tubby assured her warmly, though, in truth, back then all the high school girls looked alike in their school uniforms with short pleated skirts (except for his own standout, of course).

Tubby laid out his case. "In fact," he concluded, "Ednan is totally innocent of this crime."

"If you're right, he still committed a car theft."

"True enough," Tubby conceded, "but look at it this way. He foiled the armed robber's getaway, so you got your man. In a way, Ednan's a hero."

They shared a laugh.

"I'll check into it," she told him.

The lawyer walked out of the courthouse feeling good. Also, Judge Hughes had told him he needed younger friends. Maybe Ms. Maricopa was a good candidate.

CHAPTER 12

Debbie Dubonnet drove to Waveland, Mississippi with her father to go to Faye Sylvester's funeral. There was a nice cemetery under the live oaks behind an old wooden chapel and a couple of blocks behind the strip malls and gas stations on Highway 90. The dearly departed had a simple coffin, hanging over a grave dug in the sandy soil. The hole was covered by a purple velvet cloth

Father and daughter parked on the grounds and walked across the recently-mowed grass. Rev. Holly was there, in a blue suit, talking to a young couple. A few mourners were wandering about, visiting and looking at old stones nearby. They wore dark glasses in the searing white sunlight. Plastic flowers dotted the graves. Spotting Debbie, the preacher broke away and came to greet her with a hug.

"It's been too long," he said. They took a minute to catch up on things, the state of Debbie's marriage and the healthy development of her son, nicknamed Bat.

Tubby asked what had become of Faye's boyfriend, the other victim he had found stretched out on the kitchen floor.

"I'm told that his brother showed up and whisked him away to Ohio." That seemed odd to Tubby since, when Faye had

75

introduced her beau, she had said he was from Hattiesburg, Mississippi. Oh well, maybe he was from Ohio but he went to school at Southern Mississippi – that could explain it.

Tubby noted the arrival of "Oily" Milhouser, a neighbor of his, and a financial adviser in Uptown New Orleans. He drifted off from the preacher to give his acquaintance a quiet hello. "What brings you here, Oily?" he asked.

"Just want to pay my respects to this lady. She was my kid's favorite teacher. She gave him a lot of help when he needed it most. Being at this school really straightened him up. There are quite a few New Orleans parents here today, I see. There's Temple Graves and his wife Birdie. There's Dr. Kabatsin and his son Carter."

He walked Tubby around. In an appropriately somber and serious manner they shook hands with all. Temple and Birdie embodied old-line New Orleans. Orderly people in fashionable pressed suits, each complementing the other, and, each one's composed silver hair similarly streaked with flashes of white. Another one, Dr. Kabatsin, was in his early middle-age, black-haired, tall, thin, and good-looking. There was an early shadow of whiskers along his jaw, but his white shirt, open at the collar, and his blue blazer were crisp. His pleasant eyes found the lawyer's when their hands met and seemed to offer friendship. His young son, Carter, had been properly outfitted for the occasion, but he looked very uncomfortable in his yellow suit, and his eyes stayed on the ground while introductions were made. "Carter plays lacrosse here at Nazarene Diggers School," Dr. Kabatsin explained. "Ms. Sylvester was one of his best teachers." The doctor had an appealing manner, Tubby thought. His eyes were creased with warmth and caring, as if he thought there might be some way he could make you feel better. The boy was sullen, as if by nature.

Also in attendance was Sheriff Stockstill. They nodded at each other. The less said to his recent interrogator, the better, the lawyer thought.

Tubby found Debbie talking to a short woman who turned out to be Faye's sister, Marina. She was in the company of a large chubby man with faint remnants of red hair who was introduced as a friend, Willie Hines.

Tubby expressed his condolences to the pair.

"She was such a pioneer," said Marina, "always looking out for troubles to solve." Hines nodded solemnly, resting his chin in his neck.

Everyone cared so much for the dearly departed. So why had somebody wanted her dead?

* * *

Marina had always felt a major attraction to her sister Faye's ex-husband, Marcus Dementhe, the powerful, always forceful New Orleans District Attorney. On the other hand, Willie Hines, her date at the funeral, was just a placeholder, though he might hope for more.

There had actually been a time when Marina had not just been a sister to Faye, but also a Sister in a Catholic Order. A year in the monastic life had been enough for her, however, and her service as a helper in a Birmingham food kitchen had left her with a distaste for the poor, so she left that all behind.

Their parents were mid-state farmers, having acreage plant-ed in beans, and Mom also sold insurance. They were Catholics, a certain strain of Germans who had come to Alabama and never succumbed to the flamboyant oratory of Protestant television evangelists. Once Marina left the order, she never wanted to set foot in a church again, but she was also aware that the sanctuary might be the best place to locate a husband. While waiting, she lived with her parents for lack of something else to do. She always envied her sister, Faye, for meeting a promising man, for having a big wedding, and for being smart.

She had felt no great sadness, a few years back, upon learning that Faye and her husband, Dementhe, who then was a rising politician in New Orleans, were getting divorced. Once upon a time Dementhe had stroked Marina's hair in a very suggestive way after a family Thanksgiving dinner on the farm, pretending to adjust her glasses. And he had once contrived to let her see him naked, climbing into his bathing suit down at the lake.

Marina had been sorry to hear that Marcus had medical problems, as he had described the circumstances of his departure from the United States for a protracted sojourn in the Caribbean, but she had kept up with him via the Internet, her main social outlet. He eventually let her know that he had returned to Alabama. And he was feeling much better and working again. It was a shame that sister Faye had such a bad opinion of him, but since she had always been so closed-mouthed about the split-up, the family could never be sure who was really to blame.

Marina concealed them, especially at the funeral, but she had feelings that had never been tapped. Of that she was sure. Marcus Dementhe, for example, though older, was a successful and respected man. A little hot to the touch, but his eyes were a pleasant cool green. Whatever Faye's problem with him, Marina thought it was probably her sister's fault. The only question was whether Marcus still thought fondly about Faye, or about Marina. But now Faye was dead.

On the other hand, Marina's escort at the funeral, Willie Hines, had entered her life by happenstance. It was at the laundromat. He had picked her pink undies off the floor and made a gentlemanly comment. It was enough to merit supper, and since then he'd been her reliable date. But as for romance, not a thing.

***

The service was short and dignified. At its conclusion, Tubby and his daughter shared a quiet, subdued journey back to New Orleans.

CHAPTER 13

Peggy O'Flarity enthusiastically promoted the party at the "Sultan's mansion," and invited Tubby to be her date. He took this as more than a casual request, since Peggy was on the board of the Arts for Veterans Committee which was to be the beneficiary of this fund raiser. He understood that it was being thrown by a newcomer in town, a mysterious foreign stranger, which is the best kind, and of course Tubby said yes. Now that he was getting over surrendering to the law, he was ready to space out a little bit, kick back, and party.

The venue was a historic building in the French Quarter, recently refurbished by Chaisson Real Estate and now occupied by a Middle Eastern throng reputed to be led by an Arab prince. Or Egyptian, or Turkish ... or perhaps the brother of a prince. Accounts varied, but everyone was anxious to find out. And to see the lavish place and the exotic strangers.

Peggy explained all of this as she carried him in her car – because she had a party parking pass – down to Canal Street and across to the nighttime traffic jam of the Quarter. The same harried Lucky Dog vendor, pushing his long frankfurter-shaped cart, passed them three times as they went stop-and-go through two crowded blocks on Bourbon Street. Finally they broke free and soon were handing the keys over to the valet, who appeared at curbside to serve them in front of the three-story building. The galleries above were afire with lights and crowded with people laughing and calling out to friends and to tourists on the street below.

The couple was admitted to the mansion by an androgynous person covered in silken robes of many colors who bowed with a simple "Ahlaan wa sahlaan. Welcome," and pointed them inward where champagne was immediately offered.

A few steps further along, a tall bearded man dressed impeccably in a blazer and gray slacks and wearing on his head a striking blue turban emblazoned with a large emerald, waited to greet them, saying, "I am so happy you could come to my home. I am Sharif Bazaar. And who are you, please?"

Peggy introduced them. Bazaar leaned over and patted her hand. "So glad you could be here in my poor palace, Ms. Peggy and Mister Tubby, and I hope you will visit us often." He also bowed slightly as he waved them along with a sparkling smile. "Have a good time," he called. "I will try to remember your names."

"Such a nice man," Peggy whispered as she marched Tubby straight ahead into a great room full of people and musicians, dancers, and waiters with trays of food and drink. To their right was another receiving line where the women of the house, and the younger people – their college-age children perhaps – greeted a queue of guests. To their left was the first of several bars.

Tubby pulled one way, his date the other. They compromised by separating, Tubby with instructions to come back soon with "the best red they have."

That was no challenge. Tubby had never seen such obscure

but expensive-looking wines at a fund-raising gala. Everything was from America, on purpose obviously. They carried private labels from the North Coast of California and the Willamette River Valley, none of which he had ever heard of. He accepted a lovely Scarecrow Cabernet in a long-stemmed glass for Peggy and a generous leaded tumbler of George T. Stagg Straight Bourbon for himself.

That was before he noticed that an adjacent table was providing special party drinks. Investigation showed that these were pre-assembled Manhattans, presented in classic wide-rimmed crystal. And also an original "Saudi Sunrise," which upon inquiry turned out to be a non-alcoholic fizzy drink based on crimson pomegranate juice. Tubby observed that mostly children were drinking this.

The Sultan Prince Bazaar wandered into the room accompanied by a pair of young attendants who struck Tubby as what eunuchs might look like. They seemed to have secreted some concoction of their own in slender mugs. There were teenagers about, copping glasses of wine. Among these was young Carter Kabatsin, whom Tubby recognized from the funeral. Nothing new there. Tubby had done the same thing when he was that age, though his opportunities had been few and far between. Also, there was a round figure whom Tubby recognized from the funeral, Marina Sylvester's companion Willie Hines. He was about to approach this gentleman to ask how he happened to be at the party, but Mr. Hines quickly disappeared in the crowd.

He reconnected with his date, and together they located the silent auction tables illuminated by stained glass windows on which soft lights from the outside courtyard were playing. Unusual items were displayed. Among these was a card offering a trip for two to Dubai aboard Etihad Airways with private living room accommodations. On the plane. Then there were four tickets to next year's World Cup. And a solid gold tea set with an inscription to 19th century British royalty. And a pair of nudes cast in bronze with the etched signature of Rodin. Here was a pair of cufflinks and a picture of Winston Churchill wearing them, and a walking cane within which was concealed a small-caliber pistol. And here...

"Can we afford to bid on any this?" Tubby asked.

"Well, I don't see a minimum price on anything," Peggy replied. She started jotting down $100 on quite a few bid slips. Tubby got into the spirit. A pair of 1810 dueling pistols? $100, he wrote.

Moving on, there was a buffet of food, and lots of it. A quick walk-past revealed oysters *en brochette*, crawfish etouffé bites on tiny round toast, a huge tuna served sashimi-style, a great brown jambalaya chock full of morsels of chicken and pork, a great roast of beef, little lamb chops each with a clever silver clasp by which to hold them, chocolates, puff pastries filled with coconut custard, and more.

"The party of the century?" Peggy asked.

"Of any century," he said.

Nayo Jones, a steamy blues singer with a big voice, was swinging on a little stage, crooning out "St. James Infirmary."

Peggy went off to check on her auction bids. Tubby angled away to one of the bars to sample a Manhattan.

Drinks again in hand, he sought her in the crowd. And there she was, talking with Dr. Kabatsin, young Carter's dad.

"How do you do?" Tubby said, handing Peggy her goblet. "We met at Faye Sylvester's funeral."

Kabatsin nodded. "Yes, I do remember." Once again, his eyes looked at Tubby's like a man with a present to give.

"Dr. Kabatsin is the Prince's brother," Peggy interjected. "In fact, he is the reason that the Prince came to New Orleans."

"No, not the only reason," Kabatsin said, laughing. "And he is not yet quite a full Prince or really a Sultan."

"No?" Tubby inquired.

"No, but he is rich enough to be a Prince. He's not the first in line, however. He has to wait a while." Kabatsin gave his friendly laugh again. "Now please excuse me, I need to see what has become of my son, with all of these girls around and all of these other temptations."

He departed, squeezing through. "What a charmer," Peggy said, her eyes sparkling.

"Quite a guy," Tubby acknowledged. "What kind of doctor is he? He seemed to want to cure me."

"Not quite, hon. He may have wanted to relieve you of your bank account. He does restorative surgery for women. And he has quite a following."

"Restorative?"

"Faces, darling. Faces and breasts."

CHAPTER 14

The party was still in full swing when they left about midnight.

"How about a cup of coffee before we get the car?" Peggy asked.

"Yeah, sure. I don't know what's open. Maybe Envie, that espresso bar on Decatur. It's a couple of blocks, but..."

"That's okay with me. I'd like to walk." They nodded politely to a small yellow-haired woman who seemed to have staked out a spot beside the front gate. She ignored them, being too intent on scoping out the place and keeping a watchful eye out for one of the guests inside – Dr. Kabatsin.

Even at the late hour, there were many people strolling purposefully along the sidewalks, circumventing the sleepy waiters who were grabbing smokes outside the back-doors of restaurant kitchens, but the night was vastly more quiet than the soiree they were leaving.

Neither of them tried to talk. Tubby touched her elbow as they crossed streets and stepped over the legs of abandoned souls splayed out in doorways. There was a crescent moon, sliding in and out of clouds and hiding behind the roofs of the faded stuccoed Spanish townhouses. From the open upstairs windows, curtains blew out over the balconies and flapped like sails in the wind. As always, there was the haunting moan of ships' horns, the smells of the river, of coffee and of pot, and snatches of song from the bands playing on busier blocks nearby.

"Nice night," Tubby remarked.

"I guess," he thought he heard her say. She was strangely distant.

They came out on a crowded corner, where cars were crammed up, trying to get around a taxi. The doors of their coffee shop stood open. It was, in fact, blindingly bright inside.

Peggy found a quiet table by an open bay window, and Tubby went to the old wooden counter, covered in teas, cups, and advertisements for yoga lessons, to place their orders. Latte with soy for her and a coffee, black, for him.

Delivering these back to their little perch, he took his seat. Peggy was staring outside at the sidewalk, called by some the banquette. Young people wearing knit caps and yarn backpacks, one with "Columbia, SA" stitched on it, walked by laughing.

"Great party," he said, to start the conversation.

Peggy only nodded, mesmerized by whatever she was staring at beyond the portal. "So many colors," she said at last. Tubby was relieved to hear her speak.

She turned to face him. Her eyes narrowed. "So, where were you exactly?" she asked.

"I was just over in Mississippi," he replied, sipping his coffee.

"That's what you said." She lifted her cup and blew over it.

"I had some business over there."

"Really?" She arched her eyebrows.

"Yeah. The truth is, I needed to see a lady." To himself he

thought, *I don't need to tell her this. That lady is dead.* But the urge to be honest won out. "She was a woman I used to be serious about," Tubby continued. He took a swallow of coffee and choked.

"Take it easy," she advised.

"Right," he said, recovering. "Anyhow, Peggy, the thing is, what you and I have is becoming, uh, very important to me, and to be fair to us both I felt like I needed to clear away some old baggage."

"So that's what you did for two weeks?" Her latte was probably getting cold.

"No, for most of that time I was just camping out and lying in a tube on a creek looking up at the sky, because I was trying to figure out about all that stuff. And some other things."

"Other things?"

"Well, some things about me, but we don't need to go into that right now. The important part is I decided to go see this person."

"So, you saw her? And did those old embers get fanned?" Peggy had a very pretty face, in Tubby's opinion. High cheek bones, a healthy complexion, full lips and green-blue eyes framed in nearly-red blond hair that she had pulled back. But at the moment, she was showing more than a little strain.

"No, of course not. Actually she had a boyfriend with her when I dropped by her house, so not a lot got said. But plainly it was all over."

"All over for you? You said you had some unfinished business. I figured it was with a woman."

"Okay, yes, in a way it was about a woman. Her name was

Faye, and I felt that I should tell her about you and, just, get that part of things over with."

"How did it go?" Peggy sat back and drank from her cup of foamy brew without looking at him.

"Well. She understood. Of course, I left right away. But then I went back the next day, and I discovered her body. Dead," he added.

Peggy set her cup down. "My, that's convenient, I mean, shocking." She touched her lips with her napkin. "Who did it?"

"Yes, it was quite shocking. And I am very saddened by it. But the murderer who sliced her up is not known yet. It's under investigation."

While Tubby revisited the scene in the cabin and his revulsion, Peggy averted her eyes and seemed to be studying some space immediately above his forehead.

Clearly this was more than a shocker, and Peggy had to regroup before demanding any further explanation. Tubby supplied it nevertheless. He went through the events he knew about, his camping trip, his interrogation by the sheriff, the funeral he had just been to.

After he was done, there was a long silence.

"You didn't tell me any of this while it was happening." She was stating the plain truth.

"No. I thought I should get through it by myself."

"By yourself," she repeated. Peggy took a swallow of her concoction and quickly laid it down. "I think I need a real drink," she said.

"I wouldn't mind one myself," Tubby agreed.

"So, do you feel like you ended it? Were you sure that it should be ended?"

"Absolutely," Tubby said with conviction.

Peggy looked at him skeptically. "I'm very sorry she's dead. But you never told me about her."

"That's true, but neither one of us has talked a lot about our former lovers and affairs."

"I don't have very many to talk about."

Tubby shrugged.

"Okay, that's that," Peggy said with finality. "I'm ready to go."

"Sure." Tubby offered to help her up, which she didn't want, and they made a quiet exit.

"Would you like to come over to my place for that drink?" he asked as they walked.

"Hmmm," she muttered, pausing to take a deep breath of the aromas of the street, sugar mixed with coffee. "No. I think I'd rather stay tonight at my apartment. I can drop you off at your house if you like."

They continued on to the Sultan's mansion, where Tubby summoned her car. Loud music, maybe Kermit Ruffins, escaped through the walls.

"Hop in," she said, when he tipped the man and opened her door.

"No, thanks, Peggy. I'll take a cab."

She nodded and raised the window.

"Tough luck," the valet told him.

Tubby gave him a grin, the kind that scares people off, and walked down the street. There were at least seventeen bars between this corner and a cab stand.

91

CHAPTER 15

Marcus Dementhe, the former Orleans Parish District Attorney, had long felt the burn of his own internal corruption and had spent a lifetime trying to appease the flames by accusing others of being more corrupt than he was. As a politician, he had successfully campaigned against public greed and graft, pointing the finger at his predecessor, who was actually a trusty Boy Scout; at his political opponents; and at other lawyers and judges, often with no more factual basis than his own hungry suspicions. He was popular with voters, emotional stability never having been a requirement for electing New Orleans DAs.

But even with the immense power of prosecution in his hands, Dementhe could not resist the compulsion to overwhelm innocent women with a violence he could not control.

When he was politely examined by a policeman, one Johnny Vodka, about how his fingerprints came to be found at a rape scene, the prey-seeking public servant knew he had an entanglement from which he might not escape. Since he was nearing the end of his term, he feigned a heart condition and took a medical leave. In the confusion following Katrina, he announced that he would not be running for re-election and slipped away quietly to St. Lucia, a lovely French island in the Lesser Antilles.

So many records were lost, so many unsettled matters were forgotten in the storm's aftermath. And in time Dementhe realized that no one was looking for him. His state disability check was forwarded regularly to the island every month. Unfortunately, it didn't go as far as he would like. After a few years, while he was scheming to stage a slip and fall at one of the beachside resorts, he got into a small scrape involving the nubile daughter of a tourist.

Dementhe decided he might do better back in the States. He still had his Louisiana bar license and another for Alabama, having been raised in Anniston, and the timely death of his mother, bless her heart, had left him with some capital. So he bought an extremely nice condo in Orchard Beach, and back to the USA he went.

He hung out a shingle on his condo door, in a quiet and understated way, and presented himself to the local bar as a mild-mannered, handsome, avuncular fellow, semi-retired but wise, with the excellent experience of being the former chief prosecutor in Orleans Parish, Louisiana. That was impressive, and soon he began receiving appointments from the bench to represent indigent litigants. He accepted these commitments graciously, almost as a favor to the bar, and generally obliged everyone (except his clients) by pleading the defendants guilty.

As temporary vacancies arose in a court due to a judge's illness or some conflict of interest, Dementhe began accepting friendly assignments to sit in on an interim basis. First the city court of Gulf Shores, handling rent disputes, apartment break-ins, and drunk college students, and then the county court of

Harrison County, where he got to see real problems. He favored those involving adolescent sex slaves and their pimps, of which there were a surprising number there on the Gulf Coast. Many of the abusers and their abused seemed to come from Atlanta. Had they not been detained in Alabama, their next stop would likely have been in New Orleans.

Dementhe began to volunteer with the Sheriff's Department as a mentor to troubled youth. Ironically, and as luck would have it, some of these came from a program run by the Rev. Buddy Holly at the Nazarene Diggers School in Mississippi.

In a very short time "Judge" Dementhe was invited to help plan a Mobile Mardi Gras Ball, and that was really what it took to be an insider again. To build on his success, he moved to town. At night he dreamed of running for state Attorney General or even Governor. He would need a wife for that. Hopefully, nobody would spend much time talking to his old one. A potential new prospect was her sister, Marina Sylvester.

His dreams were not only about the grand future he might have. There was also a memory that too often surfaced at night. A woman cutting her own throat and hugging onto him while her blood gushed madly out of her expiring earthly form, leaving it to him to dispose of her deflating body. That image was true, he believed, though there were other frightening dreams also involving slender female forms about which he was less sure.

* * *

"It's a hell of a thing," Raisin told Tubby, "that you should be suspected of a murder."

Tubby shuddered. "What murder?"

"That woman up in Mississippi, my friend. What else are we talking about? It was probably some hunter."

Raisin Partlow was indeed an old friend, all the way back to college days. He had a good heart, and nothing really troubled it for long. He had a grizzled handsome face, curly black hair, and he looked perfectly fine on a tennis court.

"I don't guess I'm too much of a suspect. They let me go."

"Still. You want a beer or anything?"

"No, I don't think so."

"Or a glass of wine?"

"Doesn't that defeat the purpose of eating vegan food?" Tubby asked. They were having a late lunch at Mayas on Magazine, which served Latin fare, heavy on vegetarian and other food totally free of anything unhealthy, all of which was surprisingly delicious in Tubby's experience. Raisin hadn't been to the restaurant before.

"No, I don't want a drink, but suit yourself." He waved at the waiter, who quickly came over.

Raisin got his wine and was ready to order. "Is this paella good?" he asked.

Assured that it was, he nevertheless ordered Pampas, a grilled skirt steak salad with cotija cheese, asparagus, and other interesting ingredients.

Tubby gave it up and ordered a Caipirinha to drink, which had sugar and lime slices and other things he didn't know about. And he experimented with Coconut Curry Fish, which was tilapia in a yellow coconut sauce over jasmine rice.

"Swell spot," Raisin commented, looking over the walls decorated with faux-Mayan art.

"Very cozy," Tubby said. "Did you notice the paella for twenty people on the menu?"

"I did. Who has a pan that big? You know, there are a lot of attractive women in here." Many of them were enjoying pitchers of margaritas.

"Right," Tubby said. "It's a happening place."

"So, have you broken up with yours?"

"She may have broken up with me," Tubby said. "She said I've been leaving her out of the loop on too many things. And she's right."

"Like the fact that you had an old girlfriend in Mississippi."

"Yeah, but the last time I saw Faye Sylvester was years ago," he said, unconsciously fudging. "It was all over with us."

"You mean the last time before last month, when you decided to look her up again?"

Drinks came.

"Well, screw it," Tubby said. "I probably deserve to be dumped." He brushed some salt off the rim of his glass.

"You're certainly right, but you can't concede that to Peggy. Most men deserve to be dumped. If that were the test, where would anybody be? I'm obviously no exception." Raisin had been dumped about fifteen times by beautiful professional women who eventually got tired of a guy who, though always attentive, witty, and good looking, was content to be supported and determined to be free to exit stage-left at any time.

"Anyhow," Tubby began. "Maybe it's over. Maybe not. The bigger news is me finding two dead bodies."

"Nothing pretty about that," Raisin agreed. "But you have

to blot that sort of thing out, don't you, Tubby? I don't mean that you harden your heart. You've naturally got to feel it in the gut, but you've got to work with it, too. You can be sad, you can be mad, but those pictures don't have to stay in your mind every day."

"You may have said something profound, my friend."

"Wow!" Raisin exclaimed, but he was talking about the plate of chilled steak and salad that was placed before him. Aromas of the Andean alta plana filled the air.

Tubby's curry peaked in a lofty soup and had a sauce the color of buttercups. "Let it go," Raisin counseled. "You can't be weighed down by the human condition. You should, of course, have told your girlfriend. But a man has got to keep living despite the unpleasant things he sees, right?"

"Would the gentlemen care for a refill?" their waiter asked.

"And the unpleasant things he does," Raisin added.

CHAPTER 16

Two days later, Tubby learned that Ednan had been released from jail. He interpreted this to be the positive outcome of his brilliant legal defense, without any rhetorical shots even being fired. It was a great victory and an omen that practicing law was still the right job for him. Exalted and reinvigorated, he called up Rev. Buddy Holly and suggested that they drive over to Faye Sylvester's cabin to see if they could learn anything to explain her murder and point to the murderer.

"I suppose you know she has a sister, and you should get her permission," the preacher said.

"That's why I'd like you along," Tubby told him.

"To ask her?"

"No. As an excuse not to."

Two hours later, they were bouncing up a dirt road in Holly's Frontier pick-up, on their way to Sylvester's cabin. Holly had called the sister anyway, but she hadn't answered her phone. They half-expected to find her at the end of the driveway, but the cabin stood silent and empty in the dense pine woods.

The front door was locked, but Tubby had that problem taken care of before Holly climbed the steps.

The house was still full of the odors of dinners cooked and a woman's domestic life. The lights still worked. Tubby strode immediately through the living room into the kitchen. The dried blood stains on the floor had been cleaned up, which meant that somebody had been inside since the sheriff and his men left.

The kitchen drawers were open, and a quick check showed that there were no carving knives about. Since the murder weapon had been a sharp object, the lawmen had probably confiscated anything matching that description.

Holly looked aimlessly though the kitchen cabinets while Tubby refreshed his memory of the layout of the place. Through the kitchen were a small pantry and a separate utility room with a washer and drier. And there was a door exiting to the back porch and yard. Off the living room were two bedrooms, one tidy and kept for visitors, he surmised. The other had clothes in the closets and cosmetics on the dresser, so it was the one Faye used. He began there.

He went through the underclothes and socks in her dresser, avoiding memories of Faye in those very garments. He checked the pockets of her jackets hanging in a closet and the pants folded neatly on the built-in shelves. In the dresser there was only a small amount of jewelry, including a simple gold bracelet he remembered her wearing at a softball game the day they met, an old framed picture of a grim couple, at their wedding perhaps, and a little scrapbook with pictures and colorings, all resembling the collections of a young teenage girl. They were the sort of mementos his daughters kept. In the bathroom, the only things that looked like prescription drugs were birth control pills.

He moved into the living room, where Holly was studying the books stacked on a tall shelf beside the fireplace. "She read mysteries," he observed. "Julie Smith. And here is a book of Bonhoeffer's. I gave it to her as a present. It doesn't look like she read it though. I don't really think we should be here," he added.

The lawyer ignored him. He gave the guest room a discreet toss and found nothing more interesting than some old Cosmopolitan magazines in a plastic bin under the bed.

Back in the living room, Holly was seated on the sofa leafing through what appeared to be a photo album.

"She got a lot of letters from her students and their parents," the preacher said. "Most are thanking her for what she taught them and her positive influence."

Tubby sat beside him on the couch and looked over his shoulder. Many of the letters were fixed in place by clear plastic sheets that adhered to the pages of the album. He could read some of the phrases as Holly flipped quickly through. Most began with words like, "Ms. Sylvester, We are so thankful that you took the time with Jody to convince him he could actually accomplish something great," and, "Dear Miss Sylvester, you were my nicest teacher in the 6th grade."

"She had a lot of admirers," Tubby said.

"Undoubtedly," Holly said, wiping an eye. "She was the best teacher I had."

Tubby wondered how attached the headmaster had been to his star teacher.

One letter was loose and fell out. He picked it up and held it up to the light. It read:

"Miss Sylvester,

"You were a real asshole. My life is now a complete shitshow."

It was unsigned. He tossed the paper to Holly. "A shitshow?" he asked.

"Hmmm, just guessing, but that could be a letter from young Carter Kabatsin, who did have some trouble and got a short suspension. But he's returned for his senior year. Or it could be from one of a dozen other boys."

"Why did Carter get kicked out?"

"He mouthed off, mostly. Nothing out of our run-of-the-mill. He got mad at his teachers and threw books around, as I recall. His father took it personally. Maybe he wrote the note."

"They both came to the funeral, right?"

"I did see them, yes."

Suddenly Tubby was very tired of being in this place. "Let's get out of here," he said.

The day had turned cloudy and a high-altitude wind was twirling the black tops of the pines.

"So, what did we learn?" Holly asked as he climbed into his truck.

"Not much, I guess," Tubby admitted. "Some students loved her, and some students hated her."

"That's part of the job description."

"Her boyfriend, the man killed with her, did you notice anything belonging to him? Any clothes? A toothbrush? Boots? A letter?"

"Can't say that I did," Holly said, starting the engine.

"Me neither."

The woods there are thick, and it would have been hard, even had they been looking, for either of these two trespassers to spot the third who was squatting uncomfortably behind a downed tree. The man got up as Holly's truck bounced away toward the blacktop. He dusted his round behind. Parting the branches and straightening out his chubby figure, he made his way to the cabin to have his own look around.

* * *

The preacher dropped Tubby off next to the lawyer's flashy Corvette parked in the school parking lot. A quick handshake, and Tubby fired off on Highway 90 headed for the Interstate. Passing the last of the casinos in a blur, he left Mississippi behind him without a thought. He was putting Faye Sylvester to final rest in his mind. The pine forests, where he had sometimes imagined a life with her, were brooding and oppressive now. As the shadows lengthened, he longed only for the bright lights of the big city.

Soon enough, he exited onto the familiar Claiborne Avenue off-ramp to his own home under the live oak trees. Where he immediately noticed Peggy O'Flarity's Mercedes parked outside. Feeling an urgency to see her, he unlocked the front door and walked quickly through the house. He found her reading an old New Yorker on the back porch. A pair of drugstore glasses were perched crookedly on her nose. She turned to smile when he appeared in the doorway, and for a minute he just stood there, admiring the view.

"Hey," he said. Had her eyes always been that green?

"Hey yourself," Peggy replied. "How are you?"

"Great, just great, everything is fine." He stepped onto the porch. "And you?"

"Well," she said thoughtfully, "I've been better."

Apprehension replaced Tubby's sense of well-being. "Right," he said noncommittally. "This has definitely been a rough couple of months all around."

She looked away. "Can I get you something to drink?" he asked hopefully.

"In a minute," she replied. "I'd like a little guidance on where we go from here."

"Well, I'm not sure I know what you mean…"

But he did. And he knew where he wanted things to go. He was missing her. He groped in his mind for some more effective words of apology. But apologize for what? Didn't he have the right to do what he damned well pleased without asking for her permission? It wasn't as if they were married… and hadn't he had enough of that, by the way?

"Mean? Well, I was a bit taken aback when you finally decided to let me know you'd been to visit an old girlfriend, quite some time after the event. Not to mention her death! What do you mean, what do I mean? How in the hell would you feel if I'd been to visit an old boyfriend and didn't even have the courtesy to let you know beforehand?"

Courtesy. Tubby was awash in courtesy. She was making excellent points.

"Look, okay, maybe…"

"Never mind." Her voice was low. He took a step toward her, afraid she going to cry. But that wasn't Peggy's style.

"I'll take that drink now," she said.

Tubby turned on his heels and went into the kitchen to open a bottle of the Chardonnay he kept for her.

She was standing when he returned, staring out the screens into his back yard. He set her wine down and walked up behind her.

Taking a chance, he slipped his arms around her waist, and miraculously, answering his prayer, her body relaxed and leaned, almost imperceptibly, against him. It was enough. He leaned down and nuzzled the back of her neck, inhaling her scent. "I'm sorry," he whispered. "Truly sorry. It was all very stupid of me."

Her body softened and Tubby gently pulled her into him and resisted, momentarily, the temptation to cup her breasts with his hands. She sighed and his hands slipped up from her waist. She did not object. He wanted her then, felt the need for her growing, as his lips, not so gently now, burned into her neck, traveling up to her ear and suddenly parting her lips as she twisted to face him.

It was all he could do not to take her then and there on his porch swing. He managed to steady himself and sweep her up in his arms. The bed in his guest room seemed miles away but as he finally laid her across it, her eyes flickered open briefly. "Welcome home," he told her.

"You're quite the fool," she whispered softly.

CHAPTER 17

It was nearly eleven o'clock the next morning when Tubby opened the front door to retrieve his newspaper. It was the sort of spring day that was so perfect you yearned for an excuse to be outside – the sun was up, the sky was blue, some early monarch butterflies fluttered from yard to yard. His pretty next door neighbor knelt, tending the first-of-the season flowers she had planted along the low wrought-iron fence that ran by her sidewalk. Her hair was tied up in a red bandana, and her baggy blue jeans were rolled high above her shapely ankles. She wiped her forehead, leaving a smudge, and waved her gloved hand at him. He waved back.

Since it was probably snowing in Boston, the superiority of New Orleans was proven by a couple outfitted in T-shirts and shorts who were walking under the trees across the street, plastic cups gripped in their hands.

A lot of people in New Orleans, Tubby noted as if for the first time, carried their drinks with them as they rambled about the town. Never get caught short, that was the ticket. But not the passerby being pulled along by her large golden-haired dog. She had both her hands full, just staying upright. All in all, a perfect Sunday morning.

He retrieved his newspaper from the yard and pulled it out of its plastic sleeve as he walked up the steps to open the door. He was enjoying one last deep breath of sweet olive-scented air when he saw the headline:

MASS MURDER IN THE FRENCH QUARTER
SIX VICTIMS OF GRISLY SLAYING
CELEBRATED NEWCOMERS TARGETED

He read the news with shock and fascination as he closed the door behind him. The Sultan and all of his entourage had been murdered. He was halfway across the living room when he reached the last paragraph.

"A 25-year-old man," the paper reported, "has been detained by police for questioning in connection with the crime. He is Ednan Amineh, whom a witness described as a handyman at the residence. No charges have been filed, a police spokesman said."

"Good God!" Tubby exclaimed. He slammed the door. "Peggy, we may need a defense fund!"

Peggy had prepared a little speech for Tubby, but with all of this excitement and Tubby's obvious readiness to bolt out the door, this did not seem like the right time to give it.

She had to admire his energy as he scrambled for his clothes and ran for his car. She would have preferred to stay in bed.

CHAPTER 18

Once again, Tubby Dubonnet made his way through the metal detectors and the other security harassments to visit his client at Central Lock-up.

Thereafter it took nearly forty minutes for the guards to find Ednan and bring him down. It seems the men were fed their lunches at 10:30 in the morning. Tubby stewed, checking the same emails again and again.

When Ednan was finally led into the room, he grinned at his visitor sheepishly through the weighty acrylic barrier.

"How are you doing?" Tubby asked through the phone.

"It's not too bad here, but this all makes no sense. They arrested me again last night, and I didn't do anything." The client cracked his knuckles and shrugged helplessly.

"What exactly didn't you do?" Tubby asked to be sure.

"Kill all them people. They were my job, you know. Why should I kill them?"

"You shouldn't kill them. Why did the police arrest you?"

"I don't know. I don't know." Ednan waved his hands in the air helplessly. "When all this happened I was in the court-yard, out in the back. I didn't know anything. I was just in the wrong place."

"Why were you even there?"

"I got a job through my cousin. He works for somebody who works for the owner of the house. And he tells me they need a landscape man. So I went over and got the job. They paid good, so why would I kill anybody?"

"What did you do, on your job?"

"I was trimming the bushes and pulling up the weeds in the flower garden," Ednan explained. "And I'd hose off the bricks in the courtyard. And anything else they told me to do."

"Who is they?" Tubby asked.

"Oh, well, there was the big boss, Mister Bazaar, but I only saw him if he sat outside in the afternoon for some tea. He was always drinking tea. There was a whole lot of women who were there, too. And some boys, but I don't know about them." He scoffed when he said 'boys.' "Those boys never told me what to do," he added.

"You were there after dark? Why was that?"

"That was every night. They have lots of lights on back there. And I was in charge of being sure they turned on. They was automatic, see, but they didn't always work. I got another job in the daytime, with my uncle in Violet, collecting rent, but me coming over at nighttime was fine for these people. They stayed awake all the time." Tubby appeared quizzical. "Really!" Ednan told him. "There was music and lights on every night, even after I went home."

"What were they doing up so late?" Tubby asked.

"Well, I don't know, but I could see…" Ednan stopped.

"See how? See what?"

"They have lots of windows in the back, and, you know, I could just see them eating, or dancing."

"And what else?"

"That's all I saw." Ednan was innocent. He didn't mention that the Sultan and his family were of late being privately entertained by strange performers doing freaky things Ednan didn't care to describe. Who would believe him?

Tubby kept at it. "How did you find out about the murders?" he asked.

"I didn't see them." Ednan shook his head vigorously. Tubby watched the bun of black hair on top of his client's head wave back and forth.

"That wasn't my question," he said.

"I was cleaning out this little shed they have back there," Ednan resumed. "There was so much trash, and old rags and junk. I was starting to clean it out and take the stuff out to the street for the garbage man. I was very busy for a long time."

"For how long."

"Maybe an hour almost."

A long time to be in a shed, Tubby thought. "So then what?" he asked.

"I heard the gate to the courtyard open, and I looked to see who it was. And I saw the sister come in. I called her that, but I don't know for sure she was a sister. I saw her come in and go into the house. Then I heard her scream. I ran in, and she was calling the police."

"She did that by herself?"

"Yes. She knew how to do it."

"Then?"

"The police came and saw me with my dirty clothes, and I had these shears and these knives from the shed, and they thought it was me."

"There were knives in the shed?"

"Yes, lots of them. Some machetes, some knives for cooking barbeque, but I wasn't touching them, and I didn't kill anybody."

Tubby got to his feet.

"Is there anything you can do to help out Peanut?" Ednan asked.

The weary lawyer had no inkling who Peanut was, but Ednan tried to give him the quick version of the plight of his jail friend. "Yeah, man," Tubby sighed as he left. "As soon as we beat your murder rap we can worry about Peanut."

* * *

"He didn't do it," lawyer Dubonnet explained to Assistant District Attorney Bianca Maricopa.

She wasn't impressed.

"This is a little more complicated than your last tale about how he stole a car and therefore enabled us to catch a robber." She was much less congenial than at their first meeting. "This is a huge crime, and your client had plenty of means and opportunity."

"Yeah, but no motive. He's a working man."

"From the Middle East. Just like the victims. Maybe a family connection? Maybe politics? And there's always burglary."

"He wasn't caught with anything."

"No, but maybe that's because the sister showed up too quickly and discovered the bodies. He didn't have time to steal."

"There was no flight or attempt at concealment."

"Maybe because she had already called 911 when he walked in on her. Otherwise she might have been his next victim."

"You have a very suspicious attitude."

"You bet I do." All of a sudden she looked more like the long arm of the law than the high school volleyball cheerleader he remembered.

"But I really need to get his bail reduced," Tubby implored. "Six hundred thousand dollars is ridiculous. He doesn't have six hundred dollars."

"Think of it as one hundred thousand per victim. Anyway, it's out of my hands. My boss is overseeing this case closely."

"His Eminence Lionel Carbonera himself?"

"Of course. Six deceased, and half of the New Orleans upper crust went to some party these people threw. This case has a very high priority."

That was some party, Tubby knew. He didn't mention that he had been there, though it was nice to think of himself as among the "New Orleans upper crust."

That famous party, he reflected, gave a lot of people a chance to see how rich the Sultan was. Or maybe the Sultan wasn't the target. He'd have to get Flowers, his private detective, to look into who all those women, the brothers, the boys were. The entourage had just appeared in New Orleans like a visit by the Cirque Soleil, and like phantoms they were all gone. Vanished – in a flash. Who took them? What about the remains? Who claimed them?

He had lots of questions, including how any of this could be an income-generator.

It was hot in the courthouse and even hotter on the street. As soon as he got in the car, he tried to get the air conditioner working. It was always hard to relax or engage in speculative reflection while a client was in the New Orleans Parish Prison. The jail was a dangerous, lousy place. A lawyer worth his hot sauce ought to be able to spring a client from that squalid dungeon. He had the phone number for Ednan's girlfriend's father and called him right away.

"Hello?" the voice was tired. "This is Dijon."

"Hi. This is Tubby Dubonnet. I'm the attorney for your..."

"Yes, I know who you are." This was a normal New Orleans voice, not a Fertile Crescent Ednan sort of voice.

"Then you may know," Tubby continued, "that he has asked me to represent him on his murder charge. Right now he is stuck in jail and has a very high bail."

"I'm aware of all that. He told me all about it."

"Good. I don't think he did it, but we need to get him out of there."

"Of course he didn't do it!" the man said with conviction. "Ednan may be dumb as a post but he's not mean."

"Well, right. The issue is, will anyone undertake to pay for his legal defense? And maybe post bail, if we can get it reduced? He suggested you."

"No doubt he did," Dijon said with resignation. "Did you know that my daughter is pregnant?"

No, Tubby did not.

"That's right. Bad timing. But we all want to get him out of this. I can come up with some money. But I'm going to have to speak to my club."

"Your club?"

"Yeah. We're benevolents. My tribe. We stick together on affairs of this nature. What's it going to cost?"

Tubby named a figure for legal fees, not necessarily reasonable but realistic. He also explained that he doubted bail would go below $250,000, which would have to be put up in Orleans Parish real estate or in cash. A bondsman would want ten percent to cover that.

"That ain't going to be easy," the father of the mother-to-be said.

"Then let's just concentrate on the attorney fee," Tubby counseled.

"I'll let you know. I see your number on this here phone." He rang off.

Okay, that was progress.

Tubby leaned back to ruminate some more. There were so many compelling issues to contemplate. That pompadour-haired, corrupt bigot Marcus Dementhe, the former district attorney and ex-husband of Faye Sylvester, was also somewhere out there lurking about. And now Detective Mathewson, though retired, seemed ready to instigate some new trouble, he was sure. Mathewson was known to have connections with that group of old Cuban exiles who were reputed to have money and firearms and some very serious agenda that was in conflict with Tubby's existence. He had once pointed a gun at this brave Detective Mathewson, but had spared his life. Would the cop be as considerate of Tubby Dubonnet if he caught the lawyer again in his sights in a private spot without witnesses? Or might he think it quid-pro-quo to trap Tubby in a murder rap as payback? That was going far afield, but this was an afternoon for deep thoughts.

* * *

Ednan had no chance of making bail, but he felt himself inching toward freedom when his girlfriend's father, Dijon, came to see him with the good news that he had raised some of the money toward the legal fees. Ednan expressed his gratitude, almost crying, and then Dijon told him that his daughter, Ednan's girlfriend, Ayana, was pregnant. At that Ednan did cry.

"I've got to get out of here," he sobbed.

Dijon looked at him stonily. "And when you do," he said, "you know what you got to do."

"Leave town?" Ednan asked.

"No, fool! You're going to get a real job!" Dijon slammed his palm down on the stainless steel counter. "You're going to do right by Ayana. And the kid."

"It's my kid? Yep. Right. I got that. And I really will, Papa Dijon."

"Papa? Wait till you two get married to call me names like that. Now, everybody's counting on you. Did you do this crime?"

"I swear I did not!"

Dijon had heard this sort of thing before from almost everyone in his Mardi Gras Indian gang, but from Ednan he believed it. Dijon was certain that it wasn't in this boy to kill anybody. Certainly not an entire family. And certainly not with a knife, since Ednan puked whenever he saw blood, even his own. The chief knew this because he had practically raised the child.

Just twenty years ago, more or less, Ednan's parents had moved to New Orleans from Iraq or Turkestan, or one of those places, to be in the "oil business." That was a local joke – they ran a convenience store that sold gas and cigarettes, one of fifty similar stores run by members of a much-extended immigrant Arab or Persian family. The store was on St. Claude Avenue, in the Lower Ninth Ward, and the family lived upstairs. They weren't high on the totem pole, not even by New Orleans standards, and they were not in the oil business, and they were not closely related to the rich part of the family. From time to time Dijon bought his gas there, and on occasion he had caught glimpses of Ednan's mom, Jewel Amineh, who was starting to catch onto Western norms to the point of exposing her face and ankles. Sometimes she smiled at Dijon, who worked at the Movato Refinery. He made good wages, both then and now. His own wife had left him alone with a pre-pubescent daughter named Ayana.

Ednan's dad died, unfortunately and unexpectedly. As the water rose and swamped the convenience store during Katrina, he suffered a heart attack under the strain of dragging precious boxes of cigarettes and canned goods upstairs. With his mother's wails in his ears, Ednan tied his father's body to a coffee table that was floating by, and he propelled it slowly to the Claiborne Avenue Bridge. A Coast Guardsman, a woman actually, accepted responsibility there and offered Ednan a cup of soup. He spurned her and dove back in to swim to the store.

In the days ahead, he and his grief-stricken mother simmered in their flooded gas station surrounded by a swirling tide of oil and indescribable things. Unlike others, they were not hungry because they had tins of meat and Green Giant creamed corn to eat, but they were cut off and hopeless.

Dijon became aware of their plight while he motor-boated through the neighborhood, and spied Jewel leaning out of an upstairs window. He puttered to her stairwell landing and offered mother and son a place to stay temporarily. Jewel accepted, but she was so modest that after her first supper at Dijon's dry house across the Industrial Canal she walked herself and her boy, wading to their knees as needed, back to the apartment over the convenience store to sleep, even though they had no electricity or running water at the time. But she consented to shower the next day at Dijon's home when he was away at work. In time, when the water receded, she found an open school for her boy.

In the natural course of things, Jewel and Dijon got married. Dijon was a Mardi Gras Indian. He was totally devoted to beads and feathers and the fine art of creating a prettier headdress every year. It helped him tremendously that his new Middle Eastern wife was extremely skillful at hand stitching. She had delicate fingers and sharp eyes and could make wide pelts of tiny beads that other members of his tribe imagined could only be fabricated by a machine. Ednan grew up watching his mother sew like the wind while his stepfather selected feathers slowly and carefully. Through a crack in the door he watched the young girl Ayana learn how to put on a bra.

Soon, Dijon introduced Ednan's mother to the Indian gang, and she became a part of its theatrical marching show. An avid dancer, though fully concealed in a robe, she was also a natural tambourine player. Never a Queen, Jewel nevertheless became a respected woman of stature, a "Second Queen." Meanwhile, Ednan and Ayana bridged their own cultural gap. The girl helped her new "brother" come to grips with America.

As for the gang, Ednan was groomed by Dijon to become its Flag Boy.

"I can't picture you as no mass murderer," Dijon told Ednan in the visitors' room of the jail. "But naturally they're going to pick the first black man they see."

"I'm not black, Uncle Dijon. I think my heritage is what they call a Semite."

The big chief looked at him somberly. "Same thing, son," he said. "Don't you forget. They're always going to be after you."

CHAPTER 19

The police identified the Sultan's landlord in no time, since he appeared on the scene in a flash. E.J. Chaisson had wanted to ascertain immediately what condition his building was in. As soon as he read about the mass homicide, he definitely wanted to know who was still alive to pay the rent. Unfortunately, he learned that there was effectively nobody left, except for one middle-aged woman who was related to the Prince. She had been away on an errand to buy candles, according to her, and she had discovered the bodies when she returned. Apparently, she spoke very poor English. She was trying to arrange passage back to her home country.

At the crime scene, E.J. found the first floor's main room to be in complete disarray. It was being worked over thoroughly by the cops. Luckily, there didn't seem to be any massive damage that would warrant the landlord, who was personally wary of policemen, remaining any longer. As he proceeded to walk out, however, he found himself bracketed between two men. One, a muscular Latin man with an earring, wearing a green T-shirt who introduced himself as Detective Vodka. The other was a taller cop whose name E.J. didn't catch.

Chaisson expressed his total innocence in general, and his

total ignorance of the facts of this case, and he pleaded with the officers to discuss all of this with his attorney, Tubby Dubonnet. The mention of that name got the cops' attention and they left the room to confer privately.

"You know, gentlemen," E.J. said when they came back, "I've got to see a guy down the street about changing all of these locks. Carry on. I'll be on my way."

They let him go.

* * *

Within the hour, Tubby was driving up Tulane Avenue to answer a summons from police headquarters. Halfway there his progress was suddenly halted by a parade occupying the middle of the street. It was some Mardi Gras Indian club that had decided to pop out from Banks Street, complete with a small police escort. They were halting traffic.

The lawyer turned off the ignition and stepped outside to lean against his car and watch. There were only about fifteen major actors, vividly outfitted as always, following a brass band. As they came around the corner and entered the avenue, pedestrians fell in behind them, even some itinerants pushing shopping carts full of their possessions.

With the Indians, there was always a mystery. Who exactly were they, and why did they do this? Why were they disrupting the city's routine on this particular day, and where were they going? Nobody except the gang really knew. An enduring mystery like this, a beautiful phenomenon that was quite familiar to city-dwellers, was what he loved best about New Orleans. It was like, why were there so many more green lizards than people?

Where did all the backyard possums come from? Why did kids in school bands compete for the chance to high-step in patent-leather boots for seven miles in a Mardi Gras parade? Why did men race in red dresses or run across town while being pursued by horned women with plastic baseball bats? Why did people hold festivals to celebrate tacos and brunch?

The Indians, and their followers, turned right on Tonti Street. A toddler in feathered regalia, accompanied by her mother, broke loose from some bystanders who were photographing her and ran after the parade. The motorcycle policeman with his flashing blue lights trailed behind, and the street was soon cleared of this colorful distraction and back to its drab reality.

Tubby got back behind the wheel and, while waiting for traffic to move, made a call to Sanré Fueres, whom everybody called Flowers. He was the private detective of choice for the law firm of Dubonnet & Associates. He was the only detective whom Tubby Dubonnet trusted. Steering uptown with one hand, dodging potholes, he told Flowers what he wanted. It was a long list.

"And see what you can find out about Marcus Dementhe," he added.

"The old district attorney?"

"The same. He's not in jail."

"Maybe he died."

"That would be a good result."

"We shall see. We shall see..." Flowers trailed off. Tubby knew that the detective was already working his computer, his busy fingers sending out little inquiries.

"And look, give me a call in about an hour. I'm being ques-

tioned at police headquarters, and they might just decide to
keep me."

* * *

The lawyer made it clear to Detectives Vodka and Daneel that
he was voluntarily submitting to be interviewed.

"I'm sure that Mister Chaisson doesn't know a thing about
this," he assured them. "He probably has the applications the
tenants mailed him when they were renting the place, and it
might tell you their banking information. That could help you.
I'll be happy to see what I can pull together."

"Yes, you do that," Vodka said, even less pleasant than he
had been over coffee at the Trolley Stop. "We may follow up
with a warrant to you, so be sure you provide us with everything."

"Of course."

"You know, Mister Dubonnet," Vodka said, sucking on a
toothpick, "I'm actually becoming quite interested in you personally."

That was bad. The lawyer put on his most magisterial face.
"Why is that?" he demanded.

The detective, who had been standing, took a seat at the
table. He gestured for Tubby to have a seat also, which reluct-
antly he did.

"Yeah," Vodka began. He took the toothpick and stuck it
behind his ear. Then he changed his mind and started to clean
his fingernails with it. He shot the lawyer a quick glance then
threw the toothpick away. "You gotta realize this," he resumed.
"You came to me with information about a crime, the cold-

blooded murder of an ex-cop named Kronke right down by the river, and it sort of sounded like the start of a confession. That was bogus, right?" His eyes searched Tubby's and found them sad.

"Then I get a call from some sheriff over in Mississippi," Vodka resumed, "Strutmeyer, or something like that, was his name…"

"Stockstill," Tubby informed the cop without inflection.

"Right. Sheriff Stockstill. About a murder over there. Somebody you knew. And they let you off. You had nothing to do with that one, right?"

"Right."

"So now we got six dead people who were slashed up pretty bad. And here you are."

"Were they all in the same room, or all over the house?"

"Funny you should ask. They were all in the same room."

"So, somebody had to get them together. The victims must have had some reason to assemble with the killer. Or maybe there were several killers who forced them all to get together."

"Those are two possibilities."

Vodka's partner, Daneel, leaned over. "How many killers were there, in your personal opinion?" he asked the suspect.

Tubby feigned annoyance. "I haven't a clue. I read about this in the papers, officer. Last night, or whenever this happened, I was at home in bed."

"It was last night, about nine o'clock," Daneel said, though Vodka frowned at giving that out. "So, can somebody back you up on that?"

Tubby's thoughts went back to visions of Peggy O'Flarity, whose shoulders he might have been rubbing at about that time.

"Yes. I can tell you her name if you need it. We were together most of the night."

"I never trust these girl-boy alibis," Daneel said.

Tubby laughed in his face. "Get real, man," he said. "We're not youngsters. She had to call her kids, and you can establish the time. I had a call from one of mine, possibly at nine o'clock. You can trace all that. We grown-up people don't have private moments. I wasn't anywhere near the French Quarter, and I don't have a thing against any Sultans or their attendees, or whatever you care to call them."

Daneel backed off. Vodka stroked his light beard and looked thoughtful.

Tubby took the chance to throw in a question. "What were they killed with?"

"A knife or a sword," Vodka said absently.

"Was it found?"

"No. There was plenty of cutlery around there, but… no."

"Were the wounds to a specific area on all of them?"

"Not really. But that's enough information for you. I want those documents about the Sultan and his harem right away. Like today."

"Okay. It may be tomorrow, but you'll get them."

Tubby stood up. Nobody stopped him, so out the door he went.

* * *

It was almost three in the morning when Raisin got back to his apartment. He had been carousing a little, listening to some late music at Le Bon Temps and playing a few games of pool. He had slight difficulty tapping the right combination into his door lock. On achieving success, he stumbled directly to his bedroom and plunked down to take off his shoes. Under the sheet, there was someone's leg.

"Yo, dude!" he exclaimed and shot back to his feet. In the moonlight coming through the window, he made out Jenny's yellow hair on the pillow. *How the hell did she get in here?* he wondered. Did she slide under the door? Had he told her the front-door combination?

Raisin flipped on the lights and shook her shoulder.

"Hey, Jenny. Wake up." At last she got up on her elbows and rubbed her eyes.

"What are you doing here?" he demanded, catching his breath.

"Where is this?" She looked around the room. "I've been here before," she decided.

"Yeah. My apartment. I'm Raisin. Remember me?"

She nodded. "I need a place to stay," she said, and yawned.

"What's wrong with your apartment?"

"I can't go there. I'm in hiding."

Raisin didn't like the sound of that. "From what?" he demanded.

Her head plopped back onto the pillow.

"Bad, bad people," she mumbled. "And I fixed 'em good."

Snoring lightly, she was gone.

Raisin shook her shoulder some more, but Jenny was out.

He went to the kitchen and poured himself a beaker of water to clear his head.

Finished, he returned to the bedroom and grabbed a blanket

127

from the closet. He slid the pillow from under sleeping beauty's head. She moaned softly.

Carrying this makeshift bedroll, Raisin exited his apartment, more awake than when he had arrived. On the way out the door he re-set the combination lock. If she ever left, at least she might not be able to get back in.

Grumpily, he made his way to the garage and the cramped seat of his diminutive borrowed automobile.

She was gone when he came back in the morning.

CHAPTER 20

Clancy's Restaurant wasn't crowded yet, but it was very noisy. Nothing new there. Since it was only six o'clock, very early by New Orleans standards, Peggy and her date were directed to a table on the main floor and didn't have to work their way past the small crowded bar, which had been jammed with imbibers since mid-afternoon. In fact, there was space to stretch out around their table and a waiter who wanted to bring them whatever they needed.

"Would you like a cocktail?" Tubby offered.

"Let me look at the wine list first," she said.

"I'll have an Old Fashioned," Tubby told the waiter.

"Shall I get that while the lady makes up her mind?"

Peggy was taking a deep breath and surveying her surroundings.

"Yes," Tubby said. The waiter went away.

"It's been a couple of years since I was here last," she commented. "It looks just about the same."

"It's been awhile for me, too. Did you notice Archie?"

Her eyes focused. "Where is he?"

He raised a finger off the white linen tablecloth to point discreetly. The football great and solid citizen of the Big Easy was with family a couple of tables away.

She tried to look over her shoulder without being too obvious.

Catching a glimpse, she sighed, "You know, I visited Ole Miss when he was the quarterback, and he was so dreamy."

Tubby was sorry he had mentioned it.

"They used to always have nice pork chops, and great fish, of course," he said to change the subject.

The waiter reappeared and Peggy ordered a Bonneau du Martay White Burgundy. "Bring us the bottle," Tubby said, and the waiter gave him a huge smile.

"I'm not sure we'll drink all that," Peggy remarked.

"Well, we're celebrating."

"Really? What are we celebrating?" She leaned back while another waiter brought them bread.

"I don't know. Getting through a lot of harrowing adventures. Like you getting almost run off the Lake Pontchartrain Causeway last fall and living to tell about it."

"That was certainly a big one," Peggy agreed. The wine came, and Tubby had it poured into her glass. His Old Fashioned appeared.

"A toast to you. A survivor." He raised his glass. She did the same, and they clinked. Tubby was avoiding any mention of the Sylvester murder.

More diners arrived and quickly filled the waiting tables. The volume of voices rose dramatically.

"But why do you say we are through all that?" Peggy asked. "It was months ago, but don't you suppose that somebody tried to hurt me on purpose? Didn't you say as much?"

"I believe that's over." Tubby's voice was rising. "I think I've taken care of that." Paul Kronke, the retired cop who had intimidated both Peggy and Tubby, was now in the ground.

"What did you say?" she yelled.

"Come closer." They each leaned over the table, heads nearly touching above the candle. "The danger to you has been taken care of," he shouted.

"Was it the murder of that woman in Mississippi that ended the threat against me?"

"Faye's death?" Tubby was confused. "No, that's entirely separate." *But was it?* He started to wonder.

"So, what happened to make me safe again," Peggy asked, "when four months ago somebody was trying to kill me?"

The waiter reappeared. "Are you ready to order?" he inquired loudly.

"Yes," Tubby said, while she said, "No," at the same time.

Obligingly, the waiter left.

"We lawyers can make problems go away. We have our tricks!" he yelled.

Otherwise, nobody could hear a word.

"They must be good ones," she mouthed at him.

To be absolutely sure that the threat to Peggy had really gone away, Tubby needed one more thing. He needed to hear it from Detective Mathewson, the scariest man who had ever invited Tubby to be his friend. The intentions of the tough ex-cop, with anger management issues, were still an unknown, but Tubby didn't tell this to Peggy.

"Here comes our waiter again," he warned. She gave the menu a quick once-over.

"I think I'll have the Oyster and Artichoke Gratin and the Baby Drum, sautéed," she announced.

"Excellent choice, ma'am," he said while scribbling. "Would you care for some crabmeat with that?"

Peggy nodded.

"I'd like the Smoked Pork Loin," Tubby volunteered, "and the Fried Oysters with Brie to start."

She crossed her eyes at him for always ordering meat, or was it for the fried food? Was he imagining things, or was she starting to act like they were married?

The waiter went away, and Peggy eyed Tubby with a glint of humor over her wine glass. She reached across the table to touch his hand.

"The other night, after the Sultan's party," she said to his ear, "I realized that I have some things I ought to tell you about, too."

"That's not really necessary. We all have a history."

"True, but I gave you grief about not telling me about an old affair – one that was apparently not so old." She raised one eyebrow at Tubby, but went on. "I also had one recently that maybe I ought to mention."

"I don't see why. Is it over?"

"Yes, it ended abruptly. Do you remember who I was with the night we first met?"

"At Janie's Monkey Business Bar?"

She nodded.

"I didn't think you were with anybody. I was there with Raisin, and you were there with some girl."

"That's it. Her name was Caroline."

"And?"

"And we were, uh, together for a while."

"You mean together-together?"

Peggy blushed.

"Well, I'll be damned," Tubby said and reached for his glass. He took a thoughtful sip.

The waiter appeared with their meals, which both diners acknowledged only slightly. Disappointed, he withdrew quickly.

Peggy played with her fork. "So, there it is," she resumed.

"Why did it end so abruptly?" Tubby asked her, ignoring his food.

"Because you came along."

Her date looked off into space. " 'Like the fella once said...' "

" 'Ain't that a kick in the head,' " she finished for him.

Tubby smiled at her. She smiled back.

"I don't see it as a problem," he said.

"You don't?"

"I can understand something like that. I mean, women are very pretty. They're understanding, and supportive, and probably listen to you more than men do. Hell, I love women."

She couldn't help herself from laughing.

"But it's in the past, yes?" he asked.

"I've only got eyes for you, big boy."

"Okay. Well, then that's settled."

"Thank you," she said and looked down at her plate.

"It does give me some interesting ideas, though." She noticed his sparkling eyes.

"You can forget them right now," she said. "Just go ahead and concentrate on dem ersters."

CHAPTER 21

Tubby walked into the Trumpet Lounge on Monday. The time was nearing five o'clock.

Bright lights illuminated the dart boards and video games crowded against the walls, but the bar itself was in shadows cast by the soft glow of several beer signs and a television turned to a basketball game. The sound was off. The hulking form bent in prayer over the scarred mahogany turned out to be Lt. Mathewson. Eyes closed, he was nodding off, and his lips nearly kissed the rim of his glass of dark beer.

Tubby took the empty stool next to him.

Mathewson didn't notice this at first, but when Tubby said, "I'll have the same as him," he came to.

"Fuck you doing here?" the retired cop asked. He roused himself and sat up straight and belligerent.

Tubby shrugged. "Fuck yourself," he said.

"You didn't shoot me," Mathewson said.

"No. I didn't want to." A beer showed up, and Tubby put some bills on the bar.

"You think I ought to be grateful to you for that?" Mathewson's gruff laugh sounded like a death rattle. He found his glass of dark fluid and drained it.

"I'm just trying to put a nail in this, buddy," the lawyer said. "Is all that over with? I mean, are we over and done? I don't shoot you? You don't shoot me? That's all in the past?"

"Why? Are you worried about me?" Mathewson bared some teeth in a smile. He had a large square head and a mustache. He looked like a wounded but still-dangerous lion.

Before Tubby could answer, they were suddenly interrupted by a young man who appeared out of thin air. His black hair was slicked back, and he had on a leather vest studded with silver. He had a couple of darts in one hand. He put his other mitt protectively on Mathewson's shoulder.

"You're the boss," he said. "Whenever you say, we're ready." It was like a devotion, or a thinly disguised threat directed at Tubby.

"We?" Mathewson asked.

"Me and my whole fucking pack, man. We are ready like you wouldn't believe."

Mathewson nodded thoughtfully. He ignored the youth and locked his eyes on Tubby's. "Over, it ain't," he hissed.

"Then I should have shot you when I had the chance," Tubby said and finished his beer. "Have fun with your little boyos." He sneered at the dart player, who opened his mouth to start something, but the big lawyer walked out of the place unmolested.

So, he concluded, Mathewson was back in the game.

* * *

The short encounter with Tubby stirred up the coals in

Mathewson's brain, and he gestured to the young man to stick around.

"What's your name, kid?" he asked.

"Albert Louis. We met like ten times. Don't you remember? The kids call you the Night Watchman."

"Albert Louis?"

"Yeah, that's my name."

"I don't remember as well as I should, my friend. But I trust you, Albert Louis. Do you know a young fellow named Cisco Bananza?"

"Sure. We was all together when you was introduced by the priest, Father Escobar. The father told us that you were the one we needed to take orders from, with Detective Mister Kronke being deceased, and all."

"That's right. It's coming back to me." Mathewson motioned to the barmaid. He turned back to business. "Do you know where the guns are, Albert Louis?"

"No, sir. That's been up to Cisco, and I guess you."

"Right. I want you to get them. Now, do you know where the money is, the treasury, or what's called the Rosary Box?"

"No. Cisco does, and I guess Father. And you."

"And there were some papers. The Papal Archives. Do you know about them?"

"I just heard something about those. I don't know what they are."

"That makes you not very special because nobody else fucking knows what they are either. But first things first. Here's what I want you to do. Go see Cisco, and get him to turn over the guns and the money to you. By that, I mean turn it over to me. How many guys have you got?"

Albert Louis looked around the bar and grinned.

"If there's some money and guns in it, I guess we've got five or six for sure."

"That should be more than enough. Cisco and his bunch are all sissies. But you bring it all to me. You understand? I'll see to it that everybody gets his share. You might have to kick some butt, Albert Louis. You heard about drain the swamp? We're the alligators who rise out of the swamp's mud."

"Yes, sir. Is Father Escobar behind this, too?"

"He told you to take orders from me, didn't he?"

"That's what he said, the night we all took confession together."

"Right on," Mathewson told him and patted the back of the boy's hand. In truth, he couldn't remember a thing about the meeting. He must have been really drunk. Maybe he was mourning the blasting away of Detective Kronke, another man Mathewson had tried to make friends with, an anger management deal suggested by his police department shrink.

"What do we do," Albert Louis inquired, "if Cisco, like, doesn't want to turn over the guns or the money?"

"Then he'll be an outlaw. You can bust his ass, dude. You have my authority to do whatever needs to be done."

"All right. I get it." Albert Louis beamed. "You're our Night Watchman, ain't that right?"

A shudder ran down Mathewson's back. The gruesome fate of the last Night Watchman remained vivid in his otherwise clouded mind.

"Don't ever say those words again, son. Understand? Don't ever say them again."

* * *

Following dark streets, the air suggestive of powdered sugar, a young man walked through the French Quarter. On broken sidewalks crossed by shadows he stumbled along, ignoring the quiet oaths and whistles of the lost, to reach the business district, no less forbidding in the small hours before dawn. He had a purpose and kept going.

A man driving a street cleaner noticed him and thought him oddly dressed. "Toga party," the workman said vaguely to himself, and he went on with his work.

Young Paraclete Bazaar didn't know exactly where his Uncle Kabatsin lived, but he did have his iPhone, an old address, and Google maps, and he had a nose for blood.

CHAPTER 22

Tubby took some time to think things over. When the phone didn't ring, when Cherrylynn was out to lunch, when he could step away from his desk, where he could recline in the red leather chair the clients used and gaze out the window, his office was an excellent place for reflection.

The morning was overcast. It had started with fog, not unusual on rainy days, which covered up almost everything below his 43rd floor window to the world. A ball of golden light radiating into the cottony mist let him know that it was daytime somewhere. Sure enough, the fog began to blow away, replaced by a bewildering quick sequence of bursts of showers followed by sunshine. Tubby could now gaze down upon the wet streets and rooftops of the French Quarter far below. Pockets of rain deluging New Orleans East, Algiers, and the lands across the river to the west came into view. The Mississippi River became visible, an ominous gray force barreling through the landscape. Struggling upstream was a slow moving push boat forcing before it a long string of barges. In the opposite direction, a fast oil tanker passed it to port, bearing toward the Gulf of Mexico. This entire spectrum of weather and the city's relentless commercial pulse went on every day, every hour, even

while the wheels of suspicion and petty conniving and devious-
ness – and murder – were silently spinning in the little minds of
the people who lived in the streets below. The people who never
looked up to see the blessings the skies could hold. But such was
the way of the big city. The people on the streets were absorbed
in mysteries of their own making, and they missed the big one –
why the world was showering them with beauty. Tubby could
hear sirens somewhere, rising and receding.

So, who was behind all the violence? Who had killed Faye
Sylvester? And her boyfriend Jack? More sirens. Maybe there
was a fire somewhere. Who had killed the strange Ottoman
man and his entourage? A doomed group of travelers who had
shown up from nowhere and briefly, like sparklers, lit up the
city? They had been strangers in these parts, and they had died
gory deaths in the spectacular manner so enjoyed by locals one
and all. And it had happened in the French Quarter, where
legends are born and rarely if ever die.

And he couldn't forget the two Vietnamese goons, the ones
Ednan was initially believed to have delivered up. No one had
yet been arrested for those crimes.

Was it a coincidence, he asked himself, while watching an
orange ray of sunlight slice through a bleak cloudbank, that he
had some personal involvement, or link, to each of these crimes?
Tubby did, in fact, believe in coincidences, but how likely were
all these?

First, Faye and the boyfriend had a relationship to him, and
also to Rev. Buddy Holly, Faye's boss and confidant. Then, that
doctor, what was his name? Kabatsin. He had shown up at
Faye's memorial service. So what? He was her admirer, for all of
the kindnesses and tolerance she had shown his troubled son.

Most of the parents were grateful to Faye, and most of her students were similarly difficult. Or else why would they be shipped off to a religious school in Waveland instead of matriculating happily at Country Day, Jesuit, St. Aug, Newman, or Trinity? But even stranger was the fact that Dr. Kabatsin was there the night of the big party and turned out to be the brother of the Sultan.

And weird, too, that Tubby had been invited to the bash in the first place, since it was not the sort of event that would normally be his cup of java. Sure, it was a fund raiser for his lady friend's charity, but no stranger could have anticipated that relationship. Nobody should be gunning for him, for that matter. Trying to frame him. That would be paranoid thinking. Yet, people were dying all around him.

It was also more than a little bit strange that his client, Ednan, was involved with the Sultan as a gardener; but that could just be why they call New Orleans the world's largest small town.

The phone beeped. It was Flowers, checking in.

"I found out a couple of things," he told Tubby. "First, that boyfriend of Faye Sylvester's was a private detective."

That was news.

"He worked for a security company in Ohio. And his real name was Jasper Nomes."

"Nomes? Who hired him?"

"I don't know yet, but I have some contacts and I may be able to get a lead on this. Another fact. The remains of the Sultan and all of his kin have been autopsied and have been shipped to their home country."

"Who claimed them and arranged all that?"

"Still working on it."

* * *

Albert Louis, the young hood, soon reported to Adam Mathewson, a.k.a. the Night Watchman, that he was making progress.

"I caught up with Cisco. You know he sells cars?"

"Sure. What's that got to do with it?" They were again at Priebus's Trumpet Lounge, which was now Mathewson's "headquarters."

"Nothing. I just never knew what he did for a living. I just seen him in church. But I got him out in the car lot where I had a couple of guys with me, and I told him I was helping you out. That seemed to freak him out. He said something about you being a homicidal maniac." Albert Louis laughed.

Mathewson hacked out a chuckle of his own. "Good," he said.

"So I told him we was taking over the money and the guns, and he acted like he didn't know what I meant. We was between some new cars, nice ones, and I kneed him in the nuts."

Mathewson nodded his head enthusiastically. "And…"

"And he said all that belonged to Father Escobar, and I said we were working for the Father, so where was the money? He said he'd have to check this out and we could meet. His guys and my guys."

"When?"

"He said this Saturday night. He's got some soccer game to go to with his kids, but we can all sit and talk about it afterwards."

"Where?"

"City Park."

"You dumb shit. He's setting you up for an ambush. There's going to be a sniper around somewhere. I'm telling you, they may not have balls, but they're sneaky."

"Not to worry, boss. We got some street fighters that can take care of a bunch of Cubans. It's kind of nice, the way it's all planned out and scheduled. You'll see. We're going to get everything you want." He paused. "Some front money wouldn't hurt," he added.

"I told you you'd be taken care of," Mathewson said. "There's a big pot of dough." Or at least there used to be. How much he couldn't say, but Kronke had hinted at millions before he got shot.

"Still," the boy spread his hands.

"Here's five hundred bucks," Mathewson said, cleaning out his wallet. "This is for a big cause, you know."

"I got it."

"And if you don't come through, I'm gonna ream the guts out of every one of you."

"I know, boss. They all know that."

Mathewson got in Albert Louis's face. "Don't let my drinking fool you," he whispered, breathing beer over the boy's chin. "I'm the meanest fucking bastard you'll ever meet, and I will cram your nuts right down your throat if anyone ain't up to this job."

"We know that," Albert Louis said, backing up. "We're going to pull this off."

"And I'm also loyal," Mathewson said, smiling. "You stick with me and you're in for life."

Albert Louis's head bounced up and down.

Mr. Priebus, the owner of the Trumpet Lounge, was behind the bar and trying to overhear as much as he could of this conversation. He liked to listen to crazy people say crazy things. That's why he had a bar. Everything in this place described a reality that was superior to the boring world outside.

When Albert Louis scooted, Priebus filled a frosted mug with beer and set it down in front of Mathewson.

"On the house," he told his customer. "Did you place your bet on the Final Four?"

"I don't gamble," Mathewson grumbled.

"What's to gamble? You just pick some names and you win or lose. It doesn't have a thing to do with facts or strategy. It's pure luck. It's a complete crapshoot. A blind monkey could do as well."

"Why do I want the odds of a blind monkey?" Mathewson asked him.

"Cause it's the most fun? And it's a huge, huge pot," Priebus told him. "You could win really, really big."

"I'll take my chances with my brains," Mathewson told him. "Even though I think I'm losing them."

* * *

The rest of Tubby Dubonnet's day was spent answering correspondence, and he packed up to leave early.

Except that the phone rang, and it was someone named Willie Hines.

CHAPTER 23

Hines had a voice smooth like cane syrup and almost as sweet.

"I'm sure you don't remember me," the voice said. "Willie Hines. I'm a friend of Marina Sylvester and I met you at the funeral."

"Right," Tubby responded. He had some recollection of a portly dude who looked like he was happy even when he was offering his condolences. That's just the way some people are.

"I'd like to talk to you if you have a few minutes, Mister Dubonnet. I happen to be downstairs in your building, right now, in a coffee shop, and I wonder if I could come up."

"Come up?" No, Tubby thought. He didn't want to spoil the good karma his office, with its view of the universe he cared about, had bestowed upon him today. "No, I'll come down to you."

He packed his briefcase, a canvas bag that was basically empty of everything except a list of his computer passwords and some old letters from his father, and locked the place up.

Hines was sitting at a tiny table facing the front of the bright space off the building lobby so he could see Tubby when he showed up. He stood and waved. Tubby nodded and went to the counter to order. He got a café au lait and watched to see if they steamed the milk, which they did. The coffee came in an oversized white china cup and he carried it to the table Hines was holding for them.

"Thanks for indulging me," the man said as Tubby got a chair under him.

"I can always use some coffee this time of the day. What's on your mind?"

"Right to the point. Right to the point. That's what I like." Hines was smiling. He had a limp tea bag hanging out of his mug.

Tubby laughed along, being in a good mood.

Hines was encouraged. "I'm a friend of Marina Sylvester."

"So you said." Tubby took a sip.

"She is mortified over the loss of her sister."

"Of course. Everybody is."

"Were Faye and you very close?"

"Funny question. Why do you ask?"

"Oh, I'm sorry. I don't mean to pry."

"Fine," Tubby said. "Are you and Marina very close?"

"Ha, Ha! Good, indeed!" Hines appreciated the rejoinder. "We've had a few dates, yes. I care about her welfare. She has had a sheltered life, a former nun and all that, and needs guidance from time to time."

The lawyer nodded and concentrated on his café. There would be a point to this eventually.

"I think I also saw you at the Sultan's party," Hines said. He pursed his smiling lips and nodded conspiratorially, eyes stretched wide as if they were in a tug or war.

Tubby rubbed his forehead. "Please get to the point, Mister Hines," he said. "The coffee's helping, but I'm kind of tired."

"Understood, sir. As I'm sure you are aware, the Sultan, who I believe was actually a Sheik Bazaar, was quite wealthy."

"I would guess. He gave quite an extravagant party. What are you, some kind of investigator?"

Hines winced. "Well, well. I'm really just an interested party."

"Interested in what?"

Hines laughed and waved a hand in the air. Tubby's eyes tracked the fluttering fingers. "I'd say I'm probably most interested in the Sheik's money and where it went. Do you have any ideas about that?"

"I can't imagine what the hell you're talking about," Tubby told him. "I don't know a thing about the Sultan or his money. And what's that got to do with Faye Sylvester, or Marina Sylvester, anyway?"

"Probably nothing," Hines said. "I'm just a curious person, that's all."

"Leave me out of it," Tubby said. "I have enough problems of my own. I don't need any of yours, the Sultan's, or Marina's." He got up.

Hines leapt to his feet. "I'm so sorry. I didn't mean to offend."

Tubby shook his head and left.

* * *

He was driving home when his phone buzzed. He dug it out and saw that it was Flowers.

"Yo."

"Here's something else. All the arrangements for shipping the Sultan and his family home were made by that Doctor Kabatsin, who turns out to be the brother."

"That much I knew," Tubby told the phone while with the other hand he steered onto Poydras Street.

"Did you know that Kabatsin also has his legal troubles?" Flowers asked. "Let me think where to start."

"Usually there's a wife."

"Right on. He has a wife who is filing for divorce and wants tons of money. And the doctor has significant debts, including to some Mississippi casinos. He has a very high income, like seven figures, but he can't pay his credit cards. He's got lawsuits and rumors."

"All doctors do."

"Sure. He's got women saying he botched their surgery, that's normal, but expensive. Worse than that, there have been hushed-up allegations from women saying he took advantage of them while they were under anesthetics, and even photographed them in the nude. And his ex-wife has people hopping all over that."

"That's too bad," Tubby said. The traffic was backed up on Tchoupitoulas Street. "Do you think that would give him a motive to kill anybody?"

"Maybe the ex-wife," Flowers suggested.

"But she's not dead, is she?"

"Not that I know of."

Tubby got through the light. "Keep on digging, baby," he said. "And check out this guy who's been showing up wherever I am. His name is Willie Hines. Other than the fact that he may date Marina Sylvester, and that he talks like he's from up north, I don't have anything else on him."

"Okay. I'll put the scope on Willie, Bill, William and Billy."

"Thanks, Flowers. My lady friend is out of town and I'm heading home for the night to just take it easy."

Tubby could picture himself on the back porch, an icy Bourbon, a soft evening breeze. Maybe scramble some eggs and gruyere cheese for dinner. Slice up a tomato and chop some of the sweet basil that was growing in a clay pot on the back steps. Maybe the phone wouldn't ring.

* * *

After dark, a man with a flabby, friendly face sidled up and sat down on the stool next to Mathewson. "Whatcha drinkin', my good man?"

The ex-cop slowly turned around. "Who are you?" he growled. His eyes were hot.

"I'm not anybody. I just hate to drink alone. Name's Willie Hines," he said and stuck out his hand.

Mathewson looked at it without much interest but finally gave it a limp shake. "I'm doing beer. Good beer," he added.

"Then I'll order us each one," Hines said, and waved at the bartender.

"No thanks," Mathewson told him. He shoved his stool back and got to his feet. With a farewell wave to the whole scene, he plodded out the door.

"What's it going to be, mate?" the bartender asked the remaining customer.

"Never mind," Hines said. He dropped a five on the bar and hustled out to see where Mathewson had gone. But the street outside was empty.

CHAPTER 24

Maybe it was Ednan who noticed it first. In reading about the exploits of his alleged crime, and hearing his lawyer explain what he was being charged with, the prisoner realized that the math didn't add up. He remembered the Sultan's household as being the Prince himself, the wife, two splendid sisters, or maybe daughters, two young sons, and the two other boys, or whatever they were. That made eight. The paper said Ednan had killed six people. That's how the charges read, too. A sister had discovered the bodies. That made seven. Somebody was missing.

Was it one of the boys? Or one of the girls? He didn't know how to raise the issue. He certainly didn't need any additional charges. So he let the matter hang, pending further developments. A bigger problem was getting along with a particular guard, who was in charge on weekend mornings. A fat slob who called Ednan "Rag Head" and "Goat Fucker."

"You'd be lucky to get a goat," Ednan said under his breath. Personally his only acquaintance with goats came from pictures in school books. He kept his observations about the guard's manhood and the unusual practices of the Sultan and his family under his hat.

* * *

The missing victim, Paraclete, had taken refuge in Dr. Kabatsin's garage, slipping in quietly before dawn. The doctor's sleek black Ferrari Modena occupied most of the space, but a door at the back led to an adjoining "pool room." It wasn't locked and Paraclete found some creature comforts there. From its windows, during daylight hours, the boy could keep his patient watch on the comings and goings to and from his uncle's large house. There was also a small window in the garage, and he slid it open slightly to let in some air. On his first day, a bony orange cat hopped through the space to keep him company. It came and went as it pleased.

The boy had inherited his father's respect for and suspicion of Uncle Kabatsin, whose actual last name could have been Bazaar if he had wished, but he had long ago discarded it. This uncle's prestige in America, his great skill as a doctor, and his secure place in the community were all legend in family lore. Paraclete was a smart boy, the one his father had groomed to succeed him, and early on he had figured out that Kabatsin had been entrusted with a lot of money, a pot that was constantly replenished with wires from home whenever the oversight of the authorities was lax. The doctor somehow was able to convert this clandestine fortune into legal United States funds.

Paraclete had a natural affinity for all things financial and had even been admitted to a Middle Eastern offshoot of the Wharton Business School. He was aware, from conversations he had overheard between his father and other uncles back home, that some questions had been raised about Kabatsin's accounting for this family treasure. Paraclete took a keen interest in the discussion since, as the eldest, he stood eventually to inherit the oversight of these assets, and because he personally believed that Uncle Kabatsin was lavishly wasting the money on his child, Carter, and on his wife, who had expensively left the doctor's home.

Carter was known to present issues. He was said to have felt neglected by his American mother and to have become a malevolent youth bound for a bad end. Paraclete was expected, by his side of the family, to dominate the competition with his younger cousin.

Paraclete's own father, however, was also part of the problem. He kept marrying, and his multiple wives kept bringing new brothers and sisters into the family, all of whom required outlays of lots of cash. Paraclete assumed that his Uncle Kabatsin, for his part, might be quite displeased with these endless dalliances. As Paraclete saw it, the sooner he got control of these moving parts, the better for him and his clan.

The ostensible reason for the Bazaar family trip to America was to investigate the possibility, with Dr. Kabatsin's assistance, of naturalizing all of the Bazaar males as American citizens, so that they could eventually be educated in the United States and pursue huge fortunes of their own. Getting such an education would, of course, be a substantial expense, and it could be expected to involve a tremendous investment of family wealth.

Yet another cause for young Paraclete's concern was that his Uncle Kabatsin might expect to inherit from his murdered brother's estate. And Paraclete, since he had survived the mass murder, would be the only man standing between his uncle and that inheritance.

On the second day, peering through the glass, Paraclete

caught a glimpse of a young woman, hair like a fountain of gold rings, slipping down the driveway and disappearing around the back of the house. She was carrying something in an apron or pack around her waist. He didn't see her go inside, and he didn't see her come out. He could not guess who she was or where she had gone.

On the third day, with not much to show for his vigil, Paraclete decided it was time to reveal himself. The plain fact was that he was tired of eating the stale nuts and crackers he had scrounged from the mini-bar in his uncle's man cave. The boy washed his hands and face as best he could at the mini-bar and popped open the door to the courtyard. Here he found his cousin Carter, a youth of his own age, apparently strangling the orange cat. Carter quickly converted his throat hold on the pet into a cuddle, but the cat sprang from his arms.

"Paraclete?" Carter asked.

"Yep, it's me."

"Didn't you die?"

"No, I didn't." Cousin Paraclete marched to the back door of the house and made his entrance. The doctor was putting breakfast dishes into the sink. He had a cereal bowl in his hand.

"Hi, Uncle 'K,'" he said. "It is me. For a visit."

The doctor's bowl clattered into the sink.

CHAPTER 25

Willie Hines's next stop was the good Doctor Kabatsin's house. He rapped on the door. A teenage boy answered.

"You must be Carter," Hines said extending his hand. "I met you at Miss Sylvester's funeral."

Carter stared at the visitor suspiciously and didn't take the hand.

"I'd like to see your father," Hines told him, still smiling. There was another youth there as well. It was Paraclete, and he quickly disappeared from the hall.

"I'll find out if my father is home," the boy said. He pushed the door, but Hines held it open a crack. When the boy left, he stepped inside. Colorful artwork, from South America, he judged, hung in the hallway.

In a minute, Kabatsin appeared. Hines introduced himself again, and said that he was a friend of Marina, Faye's sister. The doctor, though rattled not just by Paraclete's sudden arrival but also by some threatening graffiti he had just found on the walls of his study and the mysterious appearance in his desk of some of his late brother's belongings, including his brother's prized turban and highly valued heirloom emerald, invited his guest into the living room. He even offered water. Hines declined, but approached the wall. "Is that a Toulouse-Lautrec?" he asked admiringly.

"Yes it is. It's a copy, I'm afraid. The original is in storage."

"Of course," Hines said. "Very wise, from an insurance perspective. You have a lovely home."

"Thank you. What can I do for you, Mr. Hines?"

"I am interested in your brother's death."

"My brother?"

"Yes, Sultan Bazaar. And his unfortunate family, of course. Quite a tragedy."

"Yes, it certainly was." Kabatsin's face froze. "How does that interest you?"

"Absolutely. A great tragedy. I am truly sorry to hear about their demise. But there may be insurance issues here as well. I know your brother was quite wealthy."

"Who are you?"

"But his estate seems to be depleted. The most likely explanation is that his wealth transferred to you. How, I'm not sure."

Kabatsin jumped to his feet. "This is outrageous! Get out of my house!"

Hines kept his seat. "I hope you will talk with me, on a straightforward and honest basis. You see, I've been told by some of your patients that you may have taken liberties with them."

Kabatsin advanced upon Hines and grabbed the front of his shirt. He lifted the plump man out of his chair and propelled him towards the door.

"Understandable that you might be upset, doctor," Hines managed to say. "But you should talk to me. We don't want these complaints to become public, do we? I'm only interested in money."

He was tossed out onto the steps. Kabatsin slammed the door and went down on one knee, nearly passing out as he sometimes did in moments of great stress. He recovered and stood up to see his son, Carter, watching him.

* * *

Right before he went to bed, Tubby got a call from a number he didn't recognize. He answered anyway.

"This is Dijon, Ednan's stepfather." The voice was right, but a little bit not right, as if Dijon were drunk or half-asleep.

"Hi," Tubby said. "I'm glad to hear from you."

"You should be glad, or not so glad. There are spirits who can speak to us. Did you know that?"

"I've always thought so," Tubby agreed.

"Yeah, well I got 'em, and we talk whenever they want. And they say there are some conspiracies on you. So you better be careful."

"Conspiracies?"

"That's right. Conspiracies to do you in, or frame you for things you have not done. And you need to be aware of that."

"Thank you very much. Who is conspiring to do this?"

"I don't know that. Just you take care. I've got other business to attend to." He hung up.

Tubby stared at his phone and lay back against the pillow. *What the hell was that?* was all he could think. And he thought that for the next hour while he lay sleepless in bed.

* * *

The soccer game out at City Park ended about nine-thirty. Albert Louis and the five members of his pack were waiting impatiently in two pickup trucks in the gravel parking lot watching the game's final moments. Albert Louis had already spotted Cisco, sitting across the field in the stands with his wife and the other fans who were watching their high-schoolers race up and down the field. Cisco didn't seem to be enjoying the game so much. He kept looking anxiously across the grass at the trucks. There was a whistle from the referee and very quickly and quietly the families collected the young and their gear from the benches, packed them into SUVs, and headed home for the night.

Albert Louis watched Cisco, his friends, and their wives all gather. There was some dissension and heated discussion as the men tried to send the wives and kids away. It took several minutes. The upshot was that some of the dads departed down Marconi Drive and Cisco was left on the sidelines with just two of his crew in support. The car lights faded away, and the spots on the field were turned off. Albert Louis and his boys got out of their trucks.

The two sides faced off with each other behind one of the goalie nets.

"I want the money, the Rosary Box, and the keys to the guns, the Armory," Albert Louis told Cisco. "I have the authority of Father Escobar and the Night Watchman."

"I talked to Father this morning," Cisco asserted bravely. "Or tried to. He could barely wake up. But he professed his love for me, for God, and for the cause."

"He's too old to run anything anymore. That's why he selected Detective Mathewson to be the Night Watchman. And we are all working for him."

"I don't know where any money is, or any guns either," Cisco said.

Albert Louis made a sign, and his friends tackled Cisco's two compatriots, who were both in their thirties and somewhat pot-bellied. They began kicking them in their crotches and faces. The men screamed. "Give him what he wants! They're killing us!"

Cisco raised his hand to stop them. This was also the sign for his cousin, who was hiding back in the live oaks of the park, to come out waving his 9 millimeter, but the cousin was out cold, having been clocked hard with a baseball bat by one of Albert Louis's skinhead brothers, who had also been concealed in the bushes.

Albert Louis got in Cisco's face. "Give it over, shithead, or you're going to die out here on this field. I'll send your wife flowers."

Cisco was a highly-pragmatic deal-maker. He sold cars for a living. While his fellow dad's club members crawled off to nurse their bruises, he offered everything to Albert Louis, in exchange for $250,000 in cash – enough to pay off his house mortgage; and his pick of three of the antique guns, including the West German Heckler & Koch HK33 with the short recoil that he favored. There was a related grenade launcher that he wanted. On the rest, which could be worth millions, he would give up his claim.

Albert Louis, quite astonished by the numbers he was hearing, quickly agreed to these terms.

They both hoped to betray the other.

"But, once we make the transfer," Cisco said, "I'm out of this. You understand? I want to hear nothing more, ever, about the cause, the Cuban Revolution, the Kennedy assassination, whose money it is or was, where the weapons came from. Nothing, you understand?"

Albert Louis nodded. He didn't know anything about any of that crap.

CHAPTER 26

Tubby conceived a trap. He made a call to the Reverend Buddy Holly but had to leave a message with the school receptionist. He had barely settled back into his chair after getting a strong cup of Community coffee, the way he liked it, when his office phone lit up and Cherrylynn said Holly was on the line.

"Hello, preacher, how's the weather over there?"

"Sunny and breezy, like most days. What's up?" No small talk today.

"I've got some ideas about Faye Sylvester's death," Tubby said, "and I'd like you to set up a small meeting of all involved."

"Involved? I didn't know anybody was officially involved yet."

"I have my suspects, but I can assure you that you are not among them." That wasn't exactly true. "That and the fact that you are prominent in the community means to me that you would be the right person to bring the whole gang together."

"Okay," Holly said, mollified. "But who, and where, and when?"

"Faye's cabin, where she was murdered, is where. When? The sooner the better. Let's try for Friday morning. The 'who' is a pretty long list, but I've just got three names for you. Marina Sylvester, Sheriff Stockstill, and, in case there's a medical emergency, that doctor, Kabatsin."

* * *

After Holly hung up, Tubby called Flowers.

"I want to get them all talked into coming over to the Mississippi cabin Friday. I assume you can be there?"

"I can make the time. But here's some news for you. I've found Marcus Dementhe."

"Where is the son of a bitch?"

"He's sitting pretty in a condo on Government Street in Mobile, Alabama."

"Nobody knew he was there? He never got indicted or charged with anything?"

"The murder of that girl ten years ago? No, he was never charged with that. What was her name? Sultana Patel? Nope, he just disappeared after Katrina and didn't run for re-election. Maybe someone cut him a deal. I don't know if anyone realized he was stateside, but he's in plain sight. The condo is in his name and he paid good money for it three years ago. Now he's a prominent citizen and being mentioned as a candidate for public office."

"That's shocking! What does he do with himself?"

"He practices law big time. But not here. The Louisiana bar page just says 'inactive'."

"How far would you say his condo is from Faye's cabin? About an hour and twenty?"

"Possibly. Or a fast hour."

"Okay, we'll invite him to the meeting, too."

164

"You'll do that?" Flowers asked.

"No, why don't you? With him, the indirect and mysterious approach works better."

Tubby made the invitation himself to Johnny Vodka. He pitched it like this:

"Officer Vodka, I'm investigating those murders in Mississippi, and they are tied into your case, the 'French Quarter Sultan Massacre.' You want to know who did it? If so, you've got to leave the jurisdiction and drive over to the vicinity of Kiln, Mississippi. That's the deal."

"What's a kiln?"

"A town."

"What's there?"

"Everything you need to know."

"Yeah? I'm thinking you're a suspect yourself."

"That's pretty rude. Here I am inviting you to a true detective event and you put me down."

"Do you still say you have information about that police killing, the one where Mathewson was a witness?"

"I've gotten past that, detective, but why don't you invite Mister Mathewson to join our party?" That was a long shot.

"He and I don't talk every day."

"That's too bad, because he's organizing a bunch of skinheads to raise hell in New Orleans. You might want to keep an eye on him."

"That doesn't sound like one of the many assignments I have in this department."

"Not until he kills somebody."

It took a few more minutes on the phone, and Tubby got

no commitment, but he concluded that Vodka was in. Then he made some other calls.

CHAPTER 27

Friday dawned overcast and chilly, the air like a cold blanket over the woods. It was the kind of day where throats get scratchy by reflex and you dream of the islands while pulling your collar tight to keep the wind from blowing down your neck.

Like estranged relatives coming to the reading of a will, the parties arrived in their own separate cars, parked in spots that seemed to be selected to allow for a speedy escape, and eyed each other warily as they crossed the yard and approached the late Faye Sylvester's cabin.

There were two Pearl River County Sheriff Department cars, one for Stockstill and the other for his deputy. Representing the New Orleans Police Department, Johnny Vodka and Frank Daneel showed up together in a city-owned Ford, unmarked except for the blue light stuck to the dashboard with a suction cup.

Tubby was surprised to see the retired detective Adam Mathewson get out of his car. Officer Vodka must have gotten through, but Tubby could only guess why Mathewson was willing to come.

Then there were the civilians. Marina Sylvester was there,

escorted by that oddball Willie Hines. She seemed as happy as Tubby was to see the elderly and dapper Marcus Dementhe come up the steps. He looked like he was ready to protest something, but his face softened for Marina and he gave her a little hug.

Doctor Kabatsin parked his Ferrari near the mouth of the driveway so that he wouldn't have to risk riding over any bumpy gravel. He hiked to the house, accompanied by his son Carter. There was also another teenager with them, a boy with dark curly hair whom Tubby didn't know. The boy calmly looked Tubby in the eye when he mounted the steps and said, "Paraclete."

To keep it homey, Tubby had also asked Peggy O'Flarity to come along. That suited her, since she seemed to be curious about this cabin and what it might reflect about Tubby's taste in women. She may also have wanted to keep an eye on her boyfriend.

The Reverend Holly was the official greeter at the front door. Flowers was inside to show people the meeting arrangements. Tubby was claiming an armchair by the door to the kitchen. The ladies had first dibs on the small sofa against the wall to his left. Three chairs had been brought in from the kitchen and placed facing the moderator in his armchair. Kabatsin took one and Willie Hines the other. Flowers took the third, which had been positioned where he could protect Tubby's flank. The cops, the kids, Mathewson, and Dementhe got standing room only at the rear, by the front door. Flowers wanted the cops there in case they had to prevent any early departures.

There was considerable shifting around, some good-natured

and some grumbling, as they all got arranged in the room. Holly pranced around nervously. The place was fairly packed.

"One, two…" Tubby went around counting heads. "Fourteen. Well, that should be just about everyone.

"I do appreciate you all coming here on such short notice, and I'm amazed that everybody seems to have found the place without getting lost in the piney woods of Mississippi."

"Why don't you cut through all that crap, Dubonnet, and get to the point." It was Marcus Dementhe, standing in the back.

"Ah, Marcus. I remember you," Tubby said. "You were threatening me with jail the last time we met, I think."

"Maybe if I offered a benediction," Rev. Holly suggested helpfully.

That got a raspy laugh from Mathewson. "I'm particular about who I pray with, pastor," he said. "Let's skip over all that. I'd like to hear what pearls of wisdom Mr. Dubonnet is going to share with us today."

"Everybody's busy," Sheriff Stockstill added in his soft and pleasant voice. "Let's get on with the program."

Detective Vodka, burning off energy by rocking from one foot to the other, nodded vigorously in agreement.

"By all means," Tubby said and tried to get comfortable in the armchair. "Just a few weeks ago I came into this house and found two people dead. Faye Sylvester, whom I knew, and Jack Stolli, whom I didn't know."

"Did you find them dead, or are you the one who killed them?" Marina demanded from the couch. Sitting next to her, Peggy raised her hand and came within an inch of slapping Faye's sister in the face. Marina raised a warning fist at Peggy.

"Ladies," Rev. Holly protested. He crossed the room and sat between them.

"No, I didn't kill them," Tubby said. "I called the sheriff, and he was here within forty-five minutes of her death, I'd say. Whoever cut these two people had to have gotten blood all over himself, or herself. There's not really any way I could have gotten myself cleaned up in the short time before the sheriff got here. Do you agree, Sheriff?"

Stockstill stroked his chin. "You wouldn't be at the top of my suspect list, Dubonnet," he conceded.

"Good enough," Tubby said. "And then, ten days after these killings, a Sultan and his whole family is wiped out in New Orleans. And I ask myself, is there any connection? I'd like to know, because I happened to be somehow associated with both of these crimes. The murders in New Orleans occurred in a house rented from one of my friends for whom I do legal work. And the man who is accused of doing these crimes, one Ednan Amineh, happened to be an existing client of mine, and still is today. He is in the New Orleans jail for these terrible acts. And I don't believe he did it."

"Why not?" Johnny Vodka asked. "He had the opportunity and plenty of motive. Them folks was as rich as kings."

"Maybe," Tubby responded, "but there are lots of reasons why it wasn't Ednan. One is that he's not very cunning and he's not very mean, but I don't have to persuade you of that. What might persuade you is the striking similarity of the two crimes, the New Orleans murders and the two right here, right here in this house. Everyone is stabbed. Everyone is killed almost ceremonially with a knife or a dagger, maybe a small sword."

"Okay," Vodka said. "I'm listening. Who did it?"

"It's instructive to know who Jack Stolli was, the man killed in this cabin with Faye. As I'm sure Sheriff Stockstill knows, and anyone else who may have access to law enforcement data bases might know, Mr. Stolli was not really a local guy from Hattiesburg, as Faye thought. He was in fact a licensed private detective named Nomes with the N&H Agency in Cincinnati, Ohio, an affiliate of the Pinkertons and some other national chains, and a specialist in undercover fact-finding. Right, Sheriff?"

Stockstill shrugged.

"I speculate that he was here in this county to seduce Faye Sylvester, which he apparently did very successfully." Tubby's face started to get hot. "And to learn compromising facts about her. We all have our own compromising facts, don't we?" His eyes roamed the room and landed on Dementhe's.

"Who would want to make up anything bad about my sister?" Marina protested. Reverend Holly patted her knee.

"My inquiring friend Flowers can think of several people." Tubby gave his detective a nod. "But one question I asked myself is, who else besides me has some connection to both the Mississippi and the New Orleans murders?"

"What did you come up with?" Dr. Kabatsin asked. He had not spoken before. Most of the others had no idea who he was, but some had noticed his Ferrari and were therefore interested in him.

Tubby was tired of sitting. His natural presentation style was to stand up, walk around, point and gesture. The room was too small to permit him the full range of his theatrical skills, but he gathered himself up and did the best he could.

"Who is connected? Well, you for one." He pointed accusingly at Kabatsin. "Your son was one of Faye's students, and you are the brother, are you not, of the Sultan Bazaar, who was the patriarch of the family killed in the French Quarter?"

Vodka straightened to attention, and Officer Daneel put his hand where it was most comfortable – on his gun.

"Nonsense," Kabatsin said. "I hardly knew Ms. Sylvester."

"Maybe so, but you wanted to know her better. That's why you hired an Ohio detective agency to infiltrate her life and dig up some dirt on her. And the two operatives in that agency were Mister Nomes, who is dead, and Mister Hines, who is in this room. That would be the Nomes and Hines Agency, wouldn't it?"

Willie Hines just smiled and nodded.

"Who told you that I hired a detective?" Kabatsin protested.

"I think the police should be able to obtain the records that will substantiate it, but perhaps we can take care of it right now. Mr. Hines, didn't Nomes, who was pretending to be Jack Stolli, work with you, and wasn't he here to spy on Faye?"

Hines went through a routine of "well well's" and "ha-ha's," but finally he said, "Of course, sir, that's probably correct."

"He was supposed to find incriminating evidence about her? Did he?"

Hines again went through his murmuring and throat-clearing, but he eventually came up with "Not a speck of it, sir. She was as pure as snow in an Ohio cornfield."

"And you're one big asshole!" Marina shouted. "Were you spying on me, too? Is that why you've been taking me out?" She started to her feet, but again Holly eased her down.

Hines went through all the "now now's" and "tut tut's" he had and then simply clammed up.

Tubby looked sad. "And now I'm afraid that Hines is just trying to find a way to make some profit out of all these events. But there is another person with connections to each of these murders. I have to acknowledge that it is my good friend, Peggy." He nodded in her direction.

"You think I'm that jealous of you!" she shrieked gleefully. "And I could kill a whole family of potential New Orleans arts patrons? That's rich!"

"I agree, and so, my dear, I've personally eliminated you, but I had to be fair to all of the law enforcement personnel who are present and taking mental notes."

"I'm taking note that the clock is ticking, and I've got a lunch to go to with the mayor of Poplarville," Stockstill told him.

"They're shooting people right and left in New Orleans," Vodka said. "I've got to get home."

"You drove a long way to get here, Vodka. You ought to be more patient, but I'm moving," Tubby said. "The other person with connections all around is young Carter over there, and who is the guy with you, Carter? Did you say your name was Parakeet?"

"I am Paraclete," the young man said with aplomb. "I am the first son of Prince Bazaar. My family was killed. I am the one who was not killed."

Vodka's partner, Frank Daneel, laid his free hand on Paraclete's shoulder. "Who killed your folks, boy?" he asked.

"I'm not yet sure. I was asleep in the attic. My private space, and that is why I am here. But though I am sad to hear of the two people who met their unfortunate end in this house, they don't truly concern me."

173

"No, probably not," Tubby agreed. He was pacing again. "But, you know, Carter, I'd have to make you a prime suspect." The boy stuck out his chin and glared at the attorney. "And the reason is that your teacher Faye gave you a bad report. She put stuff on your school record that Buddy Holly hasn't told me about, but I'm sure he will tell Sheriff Stockstill. You might even be a degenerate young man. She was getting you kicked out of school. That might have put the whammy on your whole college career. What was it you did, Carter, to earn that bad record?"

Carter bolted, about a foot, but Stockstill's deputy held him in place.

"What was it you did, Carter, that made your father so concerned that he hired a detective to discredit your teacher?"

The boy just shook his head.

"Did you kill them with that knife, Carter?"

"No!" Carter spat out. "You're crazy, man!"

Tubby considered that possibility and dismissed it.

"I believe you," he said after a minute. "I think you may have hated Ms. Sylvester, and your dad may have gone too far by hiring a detective to make her go away, but I don't think you killed her. The guy who killed her drove a truck. I know you're old enough to drive, but your dad has a Ferrari, not a truck. The guy with the truck is you, Marcus Dementhe, you perverted piece of crap. That's who killed Faye Sylvester."

Dementhe didn't even flinch, though Marina Sylvester did. She gasped and went white, but kept her seat. Dementhe just stood tall and looked skeptical.

"Kill somebody?" he said. "Of course not. I'm a respected member of the bar."

"So am I," Tubby said. "That doesn't mean anything, I'm afraid. You hated her just because she was good and sane and decent, and because she had the brains to divorce you. You hated her because only she knew what a degraded specimen of humanity you are. That would be reason enough for you, now that you are back in the country with time on your hands, but you're also thinking about running again for public office. She was one big black mark. She was someone who could be counted on not to shut up about your cruelty."

"Cruelty. What in the world are you talking about?"

"The cruelty of young girls being raped and murdered in New Orleans years ago. One of them was named Sultana Patel," Tubby said bitterly. "Cases that Johnny Vodka never solved. Cases where your fingerprint appeared. And you know how I know you did it?"

"Entertain me."

"Because that Ohio detective Stolli or Nomes was killed with one clean stab to the heart, but Faye was carved up. You took some time with her. Did you rape her, too?"

"This is so ridiculous."

Tubby turned to the Sheriff. "Was she checked?"

"Yes," Stockstill said.

"If you can sample this guy, it will match. Either way, I wouldn't let him touch anything else in this house. If you find his prints anywhere but in this room, you'll have him."

Dementhe bolted for door. Marina dived after him. The Sheriff and his deputy collared them both.

"And you drive a truck," Tubby added. "And I bet they'll find traces of blood on some clothes when they toss your condo!" he shouted.

TONY DUNBAR

Dementhe was hustled out the door, but the party didn't
break up.

"What did he have to do with the New Orleans murders?"
Peggy O'Flarity, ever unflappable, asked from the sofa.

Tubby plopped back into his chair. "Not a thing. I was
wrong. The French Quarter killer was just a copycat. Carter?"

The boy crossed his arms.

"It wasn't you, kid. It was your father, Doctor Kabatsin."

"No!" Kabatsin yelled.

"It's the only thing that makes sense. The motive was
entirely different. The killer was entirely different, but Dr.
Kabatsin, you were aware of how Faye Sylvester died and you
decided to achieve your own goals and confuse everybody. Your
brother had something on you. You have financial difficulties.
Maybe you stole the family's money. You are being accused by
your own patients of morally-reprehensible acts. So you are the
man for the job. Only you could have gotten them all to get
together in one room. Did you drug them? Did you lock them
in and terrify them? Somehow you got them in there. You
would be very fast with a knife. You could get them all before
anyone escaped. Or maybe your brother the Sultan helped you
out. He could have ordered them to submit, and then you
could have surprised the Sultan by doing him in, too. But you
missed one. You missed Paraclete."

"I deny..." Kabatsin started, before he collapsed to his knees.

"It was you," Tubby finished, and stood back up.

"It was you!" Paraclete screamed, and pulled a jeweled knife
from his shirt. He dove at his uncle. He got the blade deep
under the ribs before Daneel wrapped his arms around the
youth and wrestled him down. Vodka dropped to the floor and

176

tried to stop the bleeding while Willie Hines, his dreams of a payday melting away, ran into the yard to get Sheriff Stockstill to call for an ambulance.

CHAPTER 28

"He's dead, folks," Vodka told them sadly, referring to Dr. Kabatsin spread out on the floor. Coming through the door, Stockstill took a look at the body and said that the ambulance was on the way.

"Who gets this one?" Daneel asked the Mississippi sheriff, meaning the young Paraclete, whom he had managed to put in handcuffs.

"I guess he's ours," the Sheriff said. "This one happened in Pearl River County. The doctor here," he pointed to the body Vodka was kneeling beside, "he belongs to you."

"Great," the New Orleans cop complained. "I've got six homicides, and now the primary suspect is dead, too."

"I thought that's the way we liked it," his partner said. "Saves a lot of work for everybody." He laughed but caught himself when he realized that nobody else thought it was funny.

"The party's over, folks," Tubby said.

"Not quite," Stockstill told them. "We'll need statements and names and addresses for everybody. But it doesn't have to be in this room."

"Why don't we all go out to the kitchen," Rev. Holly sug-

gested and started to try to usher people in that direction. Only
Willie Hines went with him.

Tubby realized that Peggy was still on the sofa. She was
seeking to offer consolation to Carter Kabatsin. The boy was
staring without much evident emotion at his father's body.
Marina Sylvester disappeared into the bedroom and returned
with a quilt to lay over Kabatsin's body. "No, ma'am," Sheriff
Stockstill said softly. "We'll have to wait for the coroner to do
that."

Not knowing what else to do, she handed the quilt to
Flowers and went out to the kitchen. Tubby's man was just
hanging about, keeping an eye on Carter in case he might share
his family's passion for unexpected knife work.

Mathewson sat down in Tubby's armchair, leaned back and
stared at the ceiling. Tubby went over to Flowers and whispered
something in his ear about looking after Peggy until they all got
on the road back to Louisiana. Flowers was already doing that,
but he just nodded.

Vodka stood up and looked at his hands, seemingly surprised that they were smeared with drying blood. He frowned
and wiped them on his pants.

Addressing Tubby, he asked, "What the hell does anything
that happened here today have to do with the shooting of
Detective Kronke last fall on the Mississippi River levee? Does
anyone know?"

"Not a damn thing," Mathewson roused himself to say.
"Nothing."

"Are you still telling me it was some African-American
woman, who happened to be armed with a 12-gauge shotgun,
who did that?"

"I can't tell you the type of shotgun, but that's the way it was," Mathewson said flatly.

"Well…" Vodka was thoughtful. "I guess we'll just have to keep looking for her." He inspected his hands again, then felt behind his ear for a toothpick.

The county doctor arrived, and an ambulance and some more sheriff's deputies. They cleared everybody – except the Sheriff, the coroner, and the body – out of the room to give their statements.

* * *

It was late afternoon when they got back to the city, Tubby and Peggy in his slick Corvette and Flowers tailing them in his big Tundra. Tubby made phone contact and organized a switch at Napoleon Avenue. Peggy hopped into Flowers' truck to go home, and Tubby headed up to Tulane and Broad to tell Ednan that he was going to get out of jail. And then he had another stop to make.

* * *

Five o'clock in the afternoon, even in late winter, meant bright sunshine bathed the city. Going through the doors of the Trumpet Lounge turned the day into night. Tubby let his eyes adjust and then made out Adam Mathewson hunched over the bar. He sat down beside the detective and ordered a beer from the proprietor.

"Made in America by Americans," Priebus proudly proclaimed as he set down the frosty mug.

Tubby shrugged. He guessed that Abita Springs qualified as America.

"You still got that gang of kids? You still working with those Cuban boys and their crazy priest?" Tubby asked, trying to warm up the mug with his palms.

Mathewson turned to stare at him, his eyes a little bleary.

"My kids aren't after you, Dubonnet. They're after the money."

"To do what with?" Tubby asked.

"To give it to me." The detective chuckled and took a pull on his beer.

"What about the cause? Defeating socialism, isn't that it?"

"Now it's just defeating liberals, Mexican immigrants and the crooked media, old man. There aren't any socialists anymore."

"Liberals? That's what you're all about now?"

"Personally," Mathewson said, returning his crimson gaze to Tubby, "I don't give a shit about any of that, except I'm not a big fan of Mexicans. I'm just after the money."

Tubby stared back. "Same question. For what?"

"Younger women, older whiskey, faster horses, more money." Mathewson drank and waved at the bar man.

"To do what with? Just sit on the beach in sunny Florida?"

"Florida's as good a place as any. Or I might stay right here. I feel the urge to spread a little more mayhem before I die. Do you ever feel that way?"

Tubby didn't answer.

"I do," the retiree resumed. "There are a lot of people and things I don't really like. Some right-thinking young hombres like I got, and I'm not talking about any Mexican-lovers, could mop out the alleys, so to speak, of some very bad people. If they had the finances and the fire-power, which they will have."

"You're a crazy, dangerous nut, you know that?" Tubby said, shaking his head.

"I think I may have mentioned that I have anger issues," Mathewson told him.

"Yes."

"My boys won't be coming after you, Dubonnet. You're a tough dude, not a bleeding heart, and I respect you. And I don't intend to give you up to Johnny Vodka."

"Great."

"Maybe I'll just save you for myself."

Tubby didn't know whether Mathewson meant it or not, but he did know he didn't want to be his friend. He paid up and left the bar.

* * *

Tubby rang up Flowers to see if he could get a phone number for the pesky Ohio detective Willie Hines. Flowers already knew it. He also had some other information.

"Do you remember those two Vietnamese kids who were knifed to death out in West End, the ones they wanted to pin on your client Ednan?"

The lawyer said he did.

"My sources tell me it's the start of a battle for turf in that community – young hotheads versus the old order."

"The old order being Bin Minney?" Tubby asked, referring to the powerful community kingpin and reputed crime boss of a large part of New Orleans East.

"That's right. Seems it was two of his boys got hit."

"Really. If that's the case, there will be a lot more violence to come."

"The district attorney has quietly appointed one of his assistants, some woman, to head up a task force."

"Maybe I know her," Tubby said.

"I didn't catch her name," Flowers admitted, "but the police are worrying about an all-out war."

"A war for the corrupt soul of the city that care forgot," Tubby said grimly.

"Yeah. Right, boss. See you." Flowers hung up.

* * *

That night, Peggy told Tubby, almost sheepishly, that she thought she needed him, in her life. It was his invitation to say it back.

"Well, you know I…" was all he managed to get out.

Peggy shook her head but gave him a squeeze anyway. "We'll work on it," she said.

* * *

Tubby made a call to Willie Himes, the interfering private detective, at the cell phone number Flowers had provided.

"So nice to hear from you, Mr. Dubonnet," Hines spouted quickly. "Marina is right here, making us a beautiful supper."

"Glad to know things are working out," Tubby told him. "I suppose I'm surprised to hear that you are still in the area, now that your client, Doctor Kabatsin, is gone, along with his fortune."

"No fortune? Is that what you hear?"

"Yes, that's what I hear."

"Yes, it is very disappointing," Hines said, "but tomorrow is another day."

"I don't actually respect you and your profession, Hines, but I do happen to know of another potential pot of gold you might be interested in."

"What's that?" Hines asked, his boisterous voice suddenly lowering to a whisper.

"It involves someone you met at the Mississippi cabin, or maybe before. He's a retired New Orleans police lieutenant named Adam Mathewson, and he hangs out at a dive named Priebus's Trumpet Lounge."

"Never heard of it," Hines lied.

"He's got a gang of dangerous delinquents, and he has, or may soon have, his hands on a very impressive pile of cash. I know your line of work involves abusing confidences and trying to enrich yourself. So you'd want to know this. It's all untraceable money, and its existence is known only to a few. There's probably a cache of valuable armaments as well, similarly abandoned, forgotten, and available."

"Do you want to hire me to go after it?" Tubby heard the hunger in his voice.

"No, sir. I want nothing to do with it," Tubby told him. "Think of it as a present to you. A consolation prize for losing the Sultan's treasure."

"And the catch is?"

"Well, if he thinks you're a liberal, he might shoot you."

185

Willie Hines had nothing to say to that.

"Or anyone he thinks is coming between him and that money. Or Mexican-lovers."

"What's a Mexican?" Hines asked.

"You may be the guy for the job. I hope not to ever see you again." Tubby hung up.

With any luck he figured, Hines and Mathewson would take each other out.

CHAPTER 29

Dijon had arranged for a private talk with his daughter Ayana in her bedroom. This rarely happened, so she knew it was something important.

"I know you're having a baby," he began, and she looked down at her lap. "That's going to change a lot of things," he said sadly. "Like graduating from high school and going to college. I know how much you wanted that."

She nodded and began to weep a bit.

"Did I ever tell you what your name means, Ayana?"

"I think maybe, once."

"Well, in case you forgot, it means 'Flower.' You're my flower, baby."

Now she was really starting to cry.

"Well," her father continued, "you can still have those things you want. I'm here to help you every way I can. But you need a man, and that baby needs a father."

She raised her chin and simply said, "Yes."

"That boy Stroker is no man, you understand me? He'll never be worth a dime, and he'll just hurt you."

Ayana started to say something, but Dijon cut her off. "You need a husband who will work, and make a living, and stay by you. And who can be a part of this family. You know what I mean?"

She did.

"And you're gonna get that diploma, and you're going to go somewhere in life. Got that?" He cradled his bawling child in his arms.

* * *

"The older you get, the more you want to get things right with your life," Tubby explained to Raisin. They were each having some Oysters Bienville followed by a good bowl of gumbo at Pascal's Manale on Napoleon Avenue uptown.

"You're obviously talking about you, not me," Raisin pointed out.

Tubby trudged on. "I mean you look to see how you're shaping up in relation to whatever guiding principles you might have. Could be the Bible, or Kant, or Justinian, or Benjamin Franklin, or…"

"Or Lena Horn," Raisin added.

"Or whatever," Tubby went on. "You start to realize that you're not going to go on forever. There will be a terminus. You have to think about how you want the final picture to look."

"Too much introspection," Raisin said. "Is that why you're never satisfied?"

"Why do you say I'm never satisfied?"

"You never look satisfied."

"Have I always been that way?" Tubby stopped eating his soup.

"I think so, even in college. You've always had some higher

ideal to strive for. But, guess what? The life you're living ain't so bad."

"Sure, that's right. But you know, as you get older you have to think."

"You have kids. That's a huge achievement," Raisin reminded him.

"Right. And they're great. But you always know you haven't done all you're supposed to do for them."

"Really. Hmmm. I don't have kids. And I haven't been married for many a blessed year. So what does that make me? Where am I on the scale of human achievement?"

"I don't mean to impose my philosophical questions on you," Tubby said, staring at the chunk of French bread he had in his hand.

"In a way, Tubby, that's one of my more interesting pursuits," Raisin told him.

"Thinking about your philosophical questions?"

"No, thinking about yours."

Tubby started to say something smart, but a sense of gratitude washed over him. It was true. Raisin had almost always been there.

"Okay," he said. "Let's forget this subject."

"You may live another fifty years, dude."

"If that's true for me, it could be true for you, too. Don't you have a girlfriend? Someone you mentioned, named Jenny?"

"No, that was just a brief affair." Raisin shrugged. "She's called to say the circus left town, and she's gone with it."

"Too bad."

"Not really." Raisin speared an oyster which he took in one bite. He worked through it, and resumed. "She was a little strange. She broke into my apartment one night and said she's done some bad things. Who hasn't? But, it's probably better that she's gone away, far away."

"What bad things?"

"Didn't say."

"When was that?" Tubby asked.

"More than a week ago, I guess," Raisin told him. "She told me she fixed 'em good." Then he added, "We didn't know each other for very long."

"She was in the circus?" Tubby asked.

"Yeah. She was a, you know, contortionist, and even a sword swallower."

"I've never seen…."

"Me neither," Raisin said, and cut the discussion off.

"Anyway, she's gone," Raisin concluded.

Tubby had other things on his mind and let it go.

"You may yet get married again," he speculated, "and have a whole brood of children."

Raisin had to laugh at that. That wasn't going to happen. "You think entirely too much, my friend."

"Searching for the foundations of that proposition, I can find none which may pretend a color of right or reason," Tubby told him.

"Huh?"

"Query Thirteen."

"Are you doing Thomas Jefferson again?" Raisin tossed down his spoon.

"What does it hurt? It neither picks my pocket nor breaks my leg."

"You are doing it! How about this? 'You ought to quit it, if you can't do nothin' wit' it.' "

Tubby just looked at him.

"Moms Mabley," Raisin enlightened him.

"I think I may take up the keyboards, or the steel guitar," Tubby mused.

"Lost me there, pard," Raisin told him.

"I guess I'm talking about things I might do, just to avoid talking about death."

"Right. The grim reaper."

"Yeah. I think I need to leave him alone for a while."

"Don't rile him up?"

"That's right. I'm on break."

CHAPTER 30

Not long after the prisoner's homecoming, there was a wedding. Ayana and Ednan were getting married. Tubby was there, along with his secretary Cherrylynn, and Flowers, and Peggy O'Flarity. And at least ten members of Dijon's gang who, because of their flamboyant feathery colorings, thought it inappropriate if not impossible to sit in the sanctuary and were instead milling about at the back until the service ended. Then they would lead the wedding party on a parade around the block, following a loud tuba, to escort the bride and groom to a rented limo which would take them away to their one-night honeymoon at the Canal Street Marriott.

The church was the Second Memorial Independent & Divisional Baptist off Rampart Street. They had a good turnout. Maybe a hundred people in the pews, and Peanut was the best man. Ednan's mother, Jewel, in a beautiful sky-blue robe, sat up front with another queen or two. The father of the bride, however, was not there. Dijon was nowhere to be seen.

He was in the back, in the pastor's private men's room, with Ednan, giving him some last words of advice.

"You will treat my daughter right." That was his advice.

"Yeah, yeah, yeah." Ednan nodded his head painfully. He

was in a borrowed tux, and the collar of the starched shirt was cutting off his circulation.

"And you will work hard and support that baby."

More grimaces and nods.

"I'll tell you this, boy. Don't you ever hang out with people with no education. People with no spirituality."

"I won't," Ednan promised.

"Don't associate with those kinds of people. They'll kill you for a dollar. Now, who's got the ring?"

"Peanut."

"And you're going to raise that baby like your own. I mean, it is your own, yes?"

"Yeah, yeah," Ednan said. He looked uncomfortable.

"You want to be the Flag Boy, huh?"

"Absolutely."

"That's good. Because you know, the Flag Boy, he's the one who always gets the flower."

"The what?"

"You'll have my flower, young man."

"I think I get it," Ednan told him. It was probably the smartest thing he ever said.

THE END

HOW ABOUT A FREE BOOK?

**Keep up to date on terrific new books,
and get a freebie at the same time!**

**First click here to join our mailing list and get
*Louisiana Hotshot!***

Confirmed grump Eddie Valentino placed the ad. Hotshot twenty-something Talba Wallis knew exactly how to answer it.

And thus was born the dynamic duo of New Orleans private detectives, one cynical, sixty-five-year-old Luddite white dude with street smarts, and one young, bright-eyed, Twenty-First century African-American female poet, performance artist, mistress of disguise, and computer jock extraordinaire. Think Queen Latifah and Danny DeVito in a hilariously rocky relationship– yet with enough detective chops between them to find Atlantis.

★★★★★ 5.0 out of 5 stars **Julie Smith's Triumphant Return**
Long time fans of Julie Smith's witty mysteries will not be disappointed by this new title. Spinning off a character from her latest Skip Langdon mystery *"82 Desire"*, Talba Wallis, this book definitely ranks up there with Smith's Edgar Award winning *"New Orleans Mourning."*

WE GUARANTEE OUR BOOKS...
AND WE LISTEN TO OUR READERS

We'll give you your money back– or a different book if you prefer– if you find as many as five errors. Or if you just don't like the book– for any reason! If you find more than five errors, we'll give you a dollar for every one you catch up to twenty. Just tell us where they are. More than that and we reproof and remake the book.

Email mittie.bbn@gmail.com and it shall be done!

A Respectful Request

We hope you enjoyed *Flag Boy* and wonder if you'd consider reviewing it on Goodreads, Amazon (http://amzn.to/19zsqt2), or wherever you purchased it. The author would be most grateful. And if you'd like to see other forthcoming mysteries, let us keep you up-to-date. Sign up for our mailing list at www.booksbnimble.com.

Want to start at the beginning?

The first Tubby Dubonnet mystery is
CROOKED MAN.

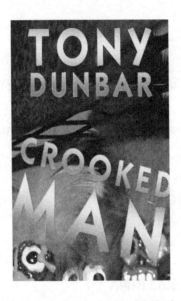

http://amzn.to/19zuVM4

What they said about CROOKED MAN:

"The wacky but gentle sensibilities of Tubby Dubonnet reflect the crazed, kind heart of New Orleans better than any other mystery series."

— *The New Orleans Times-Picayune*

"Dunbar catches the rich, dark spirit of New Orleans better than anyone."

— *Publishers Weekly*

"Take one cup of Raymond Chandler, one cup of Tennessee Williams, add a quart of salty humor, and you will get something resembling Dunbar's crazy mixture of crime and offbeat comedy."

—*Baltimore Sun*

Also by Tony Dunbar:

The Tubby Dubonnet Series (in order of publication)

CROOKED MAN
CITY OF BEADS
TRICK QUESTION
SHELTER FROM THE STORM
CRIME CZAR
LUCKY MAN
TUBBY MEETS KATRINA
NIGHT WATCHMAN
FAT MAN BLUES

Other Works by Tony Dunbar

American Crisis, Southern Solutions: From Where We Stand, Promise and Peril
Where We Stand: Voices of Southern Dissent
Delta Time
Our Land Too
Against the Grain: Southern Radicals and Prophets, 1929-1959
Hard Traveling: Migrant Farm Workers in America

About the Author

TONY DUNBAR is a lawyer who lives in New Orleans, the mirthful and menacing city in which the Tubby Dubonnet mystery series is set. In addition to the mysteries, which have been nominated for the Anthony Boucher and the Edgar Allan Poe awards, he is also the Lillian Smith Book Award-winning author of books about the South, civil rights and protest. He has an abiding interest in the Battle of New Orleans and other grand dramas in the city's colorful history and imaginative culture.

CPSIA information can be obtained
at www.ICGtesting.com
Printed in the USA
BVOW03s1325201117
500918BV00001B/2/P